ANCIENT EMPIRES

Catherine Mintz

Published by Copper Publishing 2012

www.copper-publishing.com

Cover illustration copyright rosaesther
Cover design and interior design copyright 2013
by Catherine Mintz
Copyright 2013 by Catherine Mintz

ISBN: 978-0-9839589-2-5

As bright day
Becomes black night,
It is good to remember,
They can hear,
Time to sleep,
They are near,
Safe to dream:
They are here.

Traditional evensong

The kit was quiet. The soldier sighed and shifted the little beast to what looked like a more comfortable position, where it remained, gray-faced and passive, until they bumped into another updraft. The diminutive varr took a deep breath, but Gerlac abruptly gathered its feet into one hand, and startled it to silence. "Be still," he whispered.

Yvandre peered into the man's travel-bearded face, then bared its fangs and hissed. *Do what I want to.*

The soldier grinned, and tapped it on its fierce little nose. "Shhh," he said. "Be still, pyrrin."

The kit mewed its distress anyway, convinced that if it could make itself understood, then the misery would be stopped.

Wanting a quarter paper of flash himself, the guards captain scowled at nothing, and rubbed his bristly cheeks. Serving the dark lords had given Gerlac straight teeth, a false eye that looked real and saw better, and a deep respect for the traditions of the black-and-whites. Varr's men practiced abstinence outside their own quarters.

"Oo," said the varr.

The guards captain tensed as the flyer bumped through another column of warm air. As transportation, the device was primitive beyond belief, nonsentient, mechanical, with minimal safety margins. Airbag ruptured by lightning, one had crashed yesterday, killing all on board.

The kit gagged and he patted it, absently, thinking of the live-from-the-scene coverage. For all that, he had been lucky to be detached for this solo mission. His comrades were creeping into border skirmishes on Adzak where the odds were one in twenty they would be vaporized past the point of any recoverable remains.

They said it was a painless death.

"Mft," said the kit, and the man joggled it gently.

His wouldn't be if his charge didn't survive.

It wouldn't suckle, wasn't replacing what it lost by retching. Gerlac smiled dourly, sloshed the mixture of powdered protein, sterile water, and fat in the bottle. Some said adult varr drank human blood. He'd willingly have opened a vein if it would do any good, but it wouldn't. Just another legend of the dark lords.

When he was a kid, his cousin had told him the unmen came from eggs, warmed by the light of seven moons. He'd believed that one long enough to make a fool out of himself in the barracks. The truth was embryonic varr were incubated in artificial wombs for twenty-one ten-days, then decanted and checked to insure they were true to type before they were named. Those that weren't, were culled.

"Chwuk," said the kit, reclaiming its caretaker's attention.

He gently tapped its nose again. This was a perfect specimen of its kind, named and accepted, and so the dark lords were obligated to raise it. But, thought Gerlac grimly, current politics did not dictate the job be done well. The guards captain slid a finger into one small, clawed hand, felt it clasp his, tugged gently so it could tug back.

"Chawl," said the kit.

Its gray eyes were watchful, intent. Having a silent, gestural language of their own, varr were never very verbal, but this kit was doing his best to communicate across the barriers of age and species. The man could almost see Yvandre thinking, *They use sounds, one of these must work.*

"Bript?"

"Hey, new one," said the man approvingly, and patted a fingertip on its sternum. The kit grabbed his hand, leaving beads of blood where its claws broke the skin. Gerlac worked his fingers free. Poor little creature, with its sire dead and no older clone-brothers to protect its interests, its long-term chances were slim. The black-and-white cradled it in his arms, hummed softly.

"O?"

"Ssh," he said softly. "Ssh." As a small boy, he'd cared for the youngest child while his parents and older siblings worked the fields. Being able to change a diaper and check a bottle had made him mission-qualified when Beltar hastily broke up Yesdar's household. With the old lord dead, the other varr might have turned on the old lord's un-defended kit and servitors.

The soldier had been traveling for more than five days and this was the last leg of his journey. He rocked forward and back, slowly, numb with fatigue. The local flyer went from Yost-port to Spintop Bay with intermediate stops at Ferlan, Kunst, Sithry, Varrdunost, and Klept. Sithry, famous for its dried fish, was next, and then came Varrdunost.

"Soon," he whispered to his charge.

"Oon?"

"La, la, laaa," mocked one woman, off-key, as she rocked her empty arms. The man with her snapped his fingers rhythmically in approval of her audacity.

Hands shielding the now-wary kit, Gerlac glared at the floor. On Yost, only women cared for children. If he recruited one sniggerer for the nastier chores, that would shut the rest up.

"Ssst!" said Yvandre.

The little varr would tear whomever to shreds.

On that cheering thought, Gerlac lifted the bottle from the keeper, offered it again. The kit let it drool out past the rosy curl of its tongue. A quarter shift ago, the man had made a fresh batch, hoping the problem was that the first had spoiled too subtly for his coarse adult taste to notice, but the varr refused the new as it had the old.

Plunging into a downdraft, the flyer shuddered.

"Ooo," moaned Yvandre.

Gerlac hastily patted the kit's back. Battle-hardened, he was indifferent to mess, stink, and even his own discomfort, but his charge might need help. He was not sure there was even a varr-qualified medical AI at their destination. The place was home to a scant fifty people, mostly workers skilled in managing the self-sowing plantings.

Gray eyes wide, the kit moaned, and drooled.

"Shhh," said the man, rocking forward and back. "Sssh." He pitied Yvandre, old enough to distinguish people and too young to comprehend an explanation. That didn't mean the kit didn't know enough to be scared. It was far too small to protect itself.

"Ng?"

The idiot woman laughed again, and the other passengers whispered among themselves. The man reached out, mimed feeling Gerlac's non-existent breasts, and then went suddenly nonchalant and uninvolved at the soldier's expression.

Teeth gritted, the black-and-white visualized one smooth sweep with a knife at fumble-finger's neck, the pleasant ripping sound of skin separating from flesh—

"Rrupt?" queried Yvandre.

The little creature could feel his anger, and was not sure where it was directed. The soldier made more soothing sounds, and turned his thoughts to his own position. His orders had set no term for this assignment. He might be on duty at Varrdunost for a considerable while.

They hit another rough patch of air. Yvandre gasped and spat up on Gerlac's uniform tunic. Silently cursing the illiterate who couldn't read a turbulence indicator, the soldier slapped the lock on the keeper, got to his feet, and headed for the personal. The kit convulsed again to an accompaniment of human laughter, and the black-and-white's hunched his shoulders protectively.

These townspeople seldom saw varr, had little understanding of their distant and enigmatic rulers, but even allowing for ignorance, they were more hostile than he would have expected. A bad sign, and one the dark lords' soldier would report. Yost was nearer human space than he liked, and it was possible the border was not secure.

Gerlac glanced back, thinking, *Wait until he gets a little growth on him.* He'd seen a displeased adult varr split a man open from throat to crotch: one hand, one stroke. The wretch had stood holding his steaming guts for a long moment before his brain got the message that he was dead.

Cradling the kit against the cleaner side of his tunic, the guard shouldered his way through the door at the rear of the cabin.

"Gah," said the little beast, and heaved again.

In the field, with an emergency pack, and treating a human adult, the guard knew the drill, but he didn't know what to do for the kit and he didn't trust the contents of the public medical locker.

They'd do more than skin him if Yvandre died.

The personal stank of the perfumes used to conceal the odors of elimination and sickness. Gerlac would have preferred the honest stenches. He shucked the kit's clothes off, put it into the deep, padded sink. Punching for towels and a diaper, he stripped to the waist to send his uniform tunic through the cleaner for the fourth time, and stuck his pellet-projector into the back waistband of his pants.

The figure that looked back at him from the video-plane was getting thinner on top, and permanently grim about the mouth. The left eye was bloodshot. The right, of course, never changed, although there was a piercing pain behind it at the moment. Gerlac vectored its magnification in and out, hoping the shift would reset something farther in—

"Aap!" announced the kit to its reflection, having spotted a potential acquaintance.

Sorry, fellow, thought the guard. *You're definitely the only one.*

Yvandre's tassels flared, it batted at the video-plane, then hissed at its rival and scared itself wide-eyed.

The guard blanked the screen, gathered his charge up and distracted it by turning on the lukewarm water.

The kit tried to paw the stream from the faucet, then began to piss, probably in reaction to the sound and wetness.

The man hastily set it in the sink and interposed his hand to make sure the urine went down the drain, not onto the wall, floor, and himself. Even diluted by the flow from the tap, it was easy to see the output was scanty and far too dark.

The black-and-white made a through job of washing and oiling the crotch and buttocks, then let Yvandre play with the spray for a while before he lifted it out, and swaddled it in a towel. *With any luck*, he thought, *that'll be the last time before we get there. You*, he tickled its pointed chin, *should drink something.*

"Aaahh," it said and tried to clamber up the man's bare arm.

"No," said Gerlac, and peeled it off.

"Phfitt!" Ordinarily Yvandre didn't like being thwarted, but this time it didn't argue.

The guard diapered his charge, then got yet another tube of sterile water. The kit wasn't interested in drinking but it would watch the drop form and fall—target, its mouth—and it would swallow when the man scored a hit. "Bruuum," said Gerlac, and flew the bomber in a tight circle—

The personal bumped and joggled, sending the water flying.

The frightened kit sank its claws into him and wailed, full volume.

The soldier got up slowly from his defensive crouch, one hand protecting the howling Yvandre's head while the other put up his weapon.

They were on the ground again, the last stop before their own, and the crew would be laughing their asses off. Gerlac scowled at the monitor, made a one-handed, one-gesture suggestion, and thought, *I'll be sure to mention the service in my report.* The dark lords might be indifferent to the kit's misery, might even be quietly relieved if it died, but insolence always got a varr's attention.

He remembered Joldan's expression, hands full of his own viscera.

When the guards captain finally got out of the personal, there was a new passenger in the cabin, a woman, hardly thirty, very well-dressed, lost in her own thoughts. Gerlac resettled himself, felt his freshly cleaned tunic crease and fold, thought, *They must have designed these seats to be uncomfortable, chance could never—*

The black-and-white jerked alert.

Yvandre was watching something.

The guard blinked, focused, saw the new passenger was now sitting directly across from him, staring. *Shit*, Gerlac thought, sick of amused and curious people. He shifted his charge on his shoulder and glared at her.

She flushed, looked away.

Gerlac felt abruptly apologetic. He *was* an odd sight, a fully uniformed guards captain carrying a tiny varr. Most people thought the unmen were popped from tanks and walked away, fully functioning from the moment they began breathing air, and here was one nearly as soft and vulnerable as their own offspring, for all the tassels and the tiny claws proclaimed its heritage.

The kit mewed.

"He's hungry," said the woman with the brevity of one driven to speak, but unhappy about it.

"We'll be on the ground soon," said Gerlac.

She reached for the bottle in its unlocked keeper.

"Don't," said the soldier, reaching to keep her from touching it. Burdened with Yvandre, he was too slow.

The woman plucked it out, sniffed, disapproving.

As if she can tell anything about what they feed a varr. Now he'd have to make another batch. "Listen," he said, and ground to a stop, having assumed his angry tone would be enough.

Unperturbed, she tilted the purloined bottle, squeezed a drop onto her fingertip, and tasted. Then she put her palm against the kit's cheek.

It snapped at her and howled with indignation, fully aware of who should touch it and who not.

"Please," said Gerlac, pulling away. His pellet-projector, reholstered under the front flap of his tunic, jabbed him in the gut at every dip and sway, and his orders allowed him to kill her where she sat. He had hoped to not even have to raise his voice this trip.

She flushed again, then gathered herself, rose to go, and said, finally, with awkward bluntness, "I'm in milk."

"You're offering to nurse it?" He pointed to the well-chewed nipple she had somehow overlooked, then added, "It bites."

Yvandre bared dainty little fangs, and hissed.

She proffered her ID, had had it in the palm of one hand from the time she sat down.

Gerlac took it reluctantly, wishing he'd just ignored her.

The card chirped as the list read it off and sorted its files for additional information. Pardovelman Ayana. Only child of the previous planetary governor, and, Gerlac hoped his face didn't change as he read, her husband and child had died in yesterday's flyer crash.

The guard looked at her, asking permission, but she was gazing out the window, so he pressed his list to her forearm anyway. It signaled, genome match, confirmed identity.

Embarrassed, fingers awkward on the touch pads, he ran a health-code. She was healthy, sane, and human milk, although less rich than the kit's own formula, would do. Given Yvandre needed fluids, the medical program suggested, the watery stuff might even be the better choice.

Ayana interrogated him with a look.

Gerlac nodded brusquely, and reached to drag down the privacy screen. He hated being unable to see around him, but he wasn't going to stage a show for the other passengers. Let them entertain themselves with their own imaginings.

Seeing what he was doing, the gaggle of women gave shrill little shrieks. One man gave a tongue-lolling grin and vigorously pumped a middle finger in the air, before the jade-green pigment clouding the pull-down occluded his gesture.

Shit, thought the black-and-white.

Ayana's top was a modest, wrap-around affair that could be loosened by untying the strings at the waist. The guard showed her how to block the fangs with a finger—interested, Yvandre still got in a resentful nip—but the woman simply cleaned her nipples with a practiced hand and slid the tasseled head beneath the loosened cloth.

She jumped, and then sat back, tears clinging to her lashes. The soldier winced and stared down at the treetops below, putting his right eye through its paces. *What a thing.* The man knew from watching his mother and sisters it could be pleasant to be suckled, but no human child had fangs.

Milk had stained the dark cloth of Ayana's blouse, and Gerlac wondered why she had not been medicated to dry her up. Perhaps it was too soon for her to admit the deaths. The soldier hoped she hadn't seen the official record. The man, neck snapped by the force of the explosion, must have died instantly, but the baby—

He began counting the types of foliage he could see at different magnifications. The baby, protected by its carrier and relaxed in sleep, had lived to impact the ground, might possibly have survived had the search team found it more quickly. Hidden by wreckage, it had died as its brain swelled in its skull.

Presently the first breast ran dry. When Ayana coaxed the kit off, it made a serious protest that started a susurrus of gossip beyond the pull-down. She switched it to the second nipple, stared into space and brooded, until, finally replete, the little beast stopped sucking and emerged from under the blouse.

"Pfith," Yvandre said, and was burped, expertly.

Gerlac kneaded the stiff muscles of his shoulders, and tried to think of something to say. This was a lady, and he, a one-too-many farmer's child who had to make his way in the world on his own, was no gentleman. By the time the guards captain had phrased a first, polite sentence about her destination, she was asleep with his charge in her arms.

Probably dreaming she held her own child, the black-and-white thought, and considered retrieving Yvandre. He decided against it when the kit happily bared its little fangs and flexed one clawed hand on taunt cloth. "Phfitt," said the diminutive varr possessively. *Mine.*

Feeling the kit move, Ayana tightened her hold automatically.

The soldier covered a smile by running a hand over his rough cheeks. "Shh," he barely whispered, and added silently, *I know, nice tits*.

"Naaan," said the varr, and licked its lips.

I'll ask, the man thought, *but she'll probably laugh in my face, pyrrin*.

⌐⌐

The woman had never seen the simulated land-scape she flew over in real life, but she knew it well. That fold in the billowing green was the cleft cut by the Symerill. There, where the river tumbled down from the high plains, was Varrdunost, near water for drinking and power, and provided by the riverine forest with fruit and vegetables and a good deal of the meat needed for a work force of fifty.

Pleasantly self-sufficient and virtually unde-fended, it was a prize worthy of a great deal of ef-fort. If Varrdunost could be taken for so little as a day, the riches would be incalculable. Biologicals, platinum, gold, codes, even, perhaps, in season, a varr. Her team of poachers would go prepared for that, although they had no real hope of capturing an unman.

Baron poured herself a short drink and called another file. She had been in varr territory long enough to savor the sour-sweet liquors brewed for the dark lords. Pale topaz tingling on her tongue, she stared into the tank, apparently considering the landscape sketched in light, powder, and magnetic fields and in tact remembering.

Much as she loved varr liquor, she was pierced by a sliver of terror every time she tasted it: it reminded her of the days when she had been in their territory. The unmen, protective of their own humans, could be inventively cruel to outsiders. Old Sabor said, "One smells you're not theirs, sends it wild."

Drink gone bitter in her mouth, Baron cued the file. "—sucked into pods that are blown up a bore to low orbit, then locked into the frames of crewless light-sail ships to fulfill decades-old contracts with off-planet colonies. When conditions are good, a few hundred game carcasses maybe sent up to orbit in exchange for off-planet luxuries."

A spare and elegant use of manpower, suitable for depopulated Yost. She sipped again, savoring sour, then sweet, and the final finish, indefinably bitter herbal. Fond though they were of wilderness, the varr had not done anything so crude as slaughter a worldful of people. Outraged humanity had done that trying to reclaim the planet.

"Sparsely-populated Yost requires little attention to govern." Not really listening, Baron's eyes roamed over the simulated hills and valleys. Though the dark ones seldom landed at the same place twice in a decade, Varrdunost was rumored to be an old favorite, marked more than most places by their presence.

She took another sip.

Good, if dangerous, hunting.

❏❐

The flyer planed down the runway in a cloud of spray, slid to a stop just short of the forest. The cabin hatch opened on distant thunder and the shrill song of amphibians. The soldier stood, reached to reclaim the sleeping kit, opened his mouth to ask—

Ayana rose, smoothly twisting so that her back was to him, pulled her small bag of luggage down. The soldier frowned, juggling questions. First and foremost, why was she getting off at Varrdunost? She was from Spintop.

"Hurry," she said, "they don't like to wait." Puzzled, Gerlac followed her as she carried his little lord out into the freshly washed world.

The hatch sealed behind them with a click. The flyer turned on its grapple, released, and was off, down the runway, over the trees, gone in the direction of the dark and rumbling clouds. Hand on his weapon, the guards captain surveyed his surroundings.

The place scarcely qualified as decent landing strip, even to eyes accustomed to battle zones and frontier worlds. There was a wall-less roof, meant keep the rain off or give shelter from the sun. A low stone building with a stout, locked, door. Spare parts and tools, assumed the black-and-white. Otherwise, the place was no more than a grassy clearing wet with rain.

The underbellies of the clouds were palest celadon. Reflection from the plains and the forest, thought Gerlac, as he measured the depth of color with his eye. Further in the underbrush would be sparse, but here, where sunlight could reach the ground, there was an impenetrable wall of vegetation.

"How do we get to the house?" he asked.

Ayana pointed to a gap in the trees.

It was marked by an overgrown plinth topped by a stone varr so weathered and worn it might have been mistaken for a man if the pyrrin had not held the orb and lance of power that proclaimed it a planetary lord.

"That's it?"

She nodded, yes.

Roused by her motion, Yvandre yawned and went back to sleep.

"Don't they send anyone?"

She shook her head, no.

They started walking.

Keep it simple, Gerlac told himself, and said, "I'm supposed to hire a nurse."

Ayana nodded.

"You want the job?"

"Yes," said the ex-governor's daughter, looking him in the eyes.

"Good," breathed the farmer's son. Fostering was a tricky process. One problem solved, he moved to the next, asked, "Is there a physician at the main house?"

"For us. The lords bring their own."

"Shit!" said Gerlac.

Ayana was fussing over the kit, pretending she hadn't heard.

"Let me carry it," he said, asserting his authority. "Yvandre?"

"Roo?" said the kit, suddenly alert. It sank both sets of claws firmly into the food supply, and added, "Sst!"

The black-and-white's reaching hands fell to his sides.

Ayana hid her face against Yvandre's, not quite laughing.

Shit, Gerlac thought. He was going to have to start watching his mouth. Switching the vision in his right eye, off, on, off, on in heat-mode, he asked, "How far to the house?" as he searched the surrounding trees for any signs of large life forms.

"Not far," said the soft voice.

Not helpful. "Ug?" he grunted, and vectored in on something that proved to be a mammoth, sun-warmed rock. It was going to take practice before his eye was reliable here. He hadn't worked jungle before. "Stay close." Gerlac ranged-in his pellet projector. " Get down if I tell you. Put Yvandre beneath you."

Something hoarse and avian screamed in the treetops, and the black-and-white sighted-in again, ignoring the woman's startled expression. *You'll learn*, he thought grimly. "Go on," he told her, lifting his chin to indicate the way. "Whatever happens, shield him."

They started walking again, Gerlac watching everywhere, nowhere. *This would be a very suitable place to dispose of an inconvenience. It would be best if she understood the way things were immediately. In any case, if Yvandre dies, we die, too.*

The kit yawned and slept again.

❑❐

Using elbows and knees to inch into his stealthship, Jay wondered if he would know the varr were hunting him. Not many poachers claimed to have made narrow escapes, and the consensus was that those few were lying or victims of their own imaginations.

The only reason to be in the dark ones' territory was that fabulous amounts were offered for varr goods on the human worlds unmen once held. Still, for all the careful plans made, few poachers returned to enjoy their wealth. Varr seldom failed to locate and kill interlopers.

Folding himself into the cockpit, Jay stared at the screens. The problem that had brought him forward was not a systems failure. Outside sensors were out. The hull groaned from some external pressure. Lifting the capsule hung at his neck, the young man put it between his teeth, and waited.

There was a crunch of metal on metal.

He'd lost his gamble.

Better to kill oneself than to face the dark ones' rage.

He bit down; bitterness flooded his mouth.

⌐⌐

From Varrdunost's main courtyard it was easy to see the house was laid out to the standard plan. Without bothering to greet the waiting estate manager, Gerlac gathered up Yvandre and ran. In the forest, prudence had forced him to go slowly. Here he could make haste.

Ayana trailing far behind, the black-and-white reached the medical section with its battery of equipment, stripped the kit, placed it in the proper diagnostic bin, and entered several codes. Then, hands pressed to the consol, he watched as the machine closed in.

Yvandre screamed.

Fighting off the snaking sensors and grappling with the manipulators, the little creature protested every sample, every scan. It clawed the inside of its prison and chewed at the loose lining until Ayana, afraid it would choke, had the soldier pull the stuff from its talons and teeth.

By the time the machine was satisfied, Yvandre was hysterical and furious. It promptly bit Gerlac when he scooped it out. The black-and-white cursed fluently, wrapped the hellion in a blanket, and handed it to Ayana, who placed it in a carrier very quickly indeed and got away with mere scratches.

Reset, the equipment treated Gerlac, too.

His wounds were a bright, healing pink when he gathered the squirming kit up and made his peace. "Ooo, who'sis? Ooo—" The man grabbed the ankles in one hand and pumped the legs up and down. "Sis Yvandre?"

"Ap!" Its fists and feet thumped against the man's chest.

"Ahhh," groaned Gerlac, obligingly.

Ayana stared.

The soldier jounced around in a circle, then asked the fierce little face. "Sis Yvandre. Hmm?"

"Ap?" The kit looked uncertain.

The black-and-white tickled a long-toed foot, got pinched, and grinned. "Sis Yvandre!"

"Broo!"

At least it didn't carry a grudge. Or maybe Yvandre was just too tired to wage war. Wait until it got older. Gerlac carried it back to the front of the house. Sleeping varr cradled on his shoulder, he apologized for his earlier breach of protocol to the still-waiting welcomers.

"Better safe than sorry," said the household manager, and he and Gerlac exchanged a look of complete comprehension. You did not serve the dark lords long if you did not please them, first, last, and always. "Pana Lodge is ready for you."

Gerlac lifted his chin in query.

"It's where the lords usually stay."

"Defensible?"

The man nodded.

Ayana looked as if she were about to speak, but didn't.

"Down there." The manager walked off without another word. Out here they seldom saw strangers and there would be no haste in getting acquainted.

"Ayana?" Gerlac said, and then stopped, uncertain how to address the lady.

She said, "Yes," firmly, and hurried toward him, carrier in her arms.

All right, he thought. *No ceremony.* He waited for her, and they started down the path to the lodge. The green world beneath the canopy was silent and their footsteps on the paved path seemed very loud.

There must be hundreds of curious eyes, thought Gerlac, vectoring his own in and out. *Some of those heat-forms must be people. The oldest children, perhaps, wanting to see the newcomers.*

"Grunk-grunk-grunk!" teased a bunch of leaves. The soldier switched cartridges and zapped, giving the soft pellet enough force to sting, and was rewarded with an entirely human yip.

Point made: don't hang around here.

One-and-a-half stories, Pana Lodge had a wide courtyard and a surrounding wall bound by roots and vines that quivered although there was no breeze. Gerlac smiled. Biological defenses. It would take some precautions to make the place completely safe for the lady and himself.

A single enormous pana tree rose near the gate, hung with pendant flowers and ripe fruit. Ayana pulled a globe as she passed, murmured thanks, and sank her teeth into rosy flesh.

The black-and-white made a mental note of what she said. He had never thanked a plant in his life and was not eager to start, but it was better not to give offense.

Watching the tree leaves ripple inquisitively, Gerlac lifted Yvandre over his head and turned about, showing the place its lord. It would shelter any varr and tolerate its servants but woe betide a stranger. For the kit, it was a very safe place.

Perhaps Beltar has acted in the varrling's best interest by sending it here. If so, then the Red Lord will expect results. On that thought, the black-and-white's estimate of the nature of his mission underwent a paradigm shift. He might be here a while. He was lucky he was young for a guards captain.

"I hope it's clean," said Ayana.

"Yes," said Gerlac, absently. He doubted the place was dirty. It would have been looking after itself. More important to him was that, walled with native stone and roofed with pana-leaf-green solar tiles, the lodge would have to be reduced to rubble before its inhabitants could be captured.

Right now they had to get into this haven.

Handing Yvandre to Ayana, the soldier put both hands into the opening by the door, and waited. Being read was always a nervous moment, for, although the dark lords would repair him, as they had when he lost his eye, the inevitable investigation into why he had set off the—

"Fiit," said their mutual charge, having spotted a scarlet po-bird among the shrubbery.

"Not now," said Ayana.

"Aaah!" yelled the little lord.

"No," said Ayana. "Not now. See what Gerlac's doing."

"Rupt!"

"Yvandre!"

Wait until it starts to walk, the guards captain thought, flexing his fingers, entering first level, second, third. *It will hunt everything that moves, and run faster than you, too.* He pressed with his shoulder and the door yielded, letting sunlight blaze on the furnishings of the main room.

Gerlac gasped, then released a slow breath full of unvoiced apologies: the tassel-framed, scarlet-lipped face was part of a mural. From where the soldier stood everything was the pale gold and silver the night-visioned varr loved.

The dark lords had made themselves comfortable here. *It's all real*, he thought, and wondered how many artisans had labored to produce the interlacing vines of the door screen, the black and white ripples on the stone floors.

"Is it clean?" asked Ayana.

He stood aside so she could see in.

"Oh!"

"Naaan," said the pyrrin, approving.

Gerlac grinned. *If my father could see me now.* "Check the bedding and the kitchen," he said. "The place hasn't been used for a couple of years, and it'll be sundown soon. Better not to have to fetch anything from the main house after dark."

Ayana was gone before he finished speaking.

Looking around him, he nuzzled the stiff hair of the abruptly transferred Yvandre, and wondered if a governor's daughter learned to cook. The mighty clatter of pots suggested she at least knew what to inspect. There was a patter of feet heading upstairs—

"Naa?" asked the kit, reaching for a golden vine.

"Naaan," said the man, and moved it closer, so it could touch.

❑❐

He stood in the leafy shadows, knowing the dark lords knew he was there. Aubry's concealment was a gesture of respect, nothing else. He needed to look at them one last time before he made up his mind. Sighing, he sank to his knees, watching as they tore at hartebuck with elegant voracity.

Designed with fangs, claws, and the short gut of the carnivore, meat-hungry varr maintain vast reserves for their solitary stalks, but when local fall comes, and the flyers float above the fields sucking the grain out of its tassels, they sometimes come to hunt together.

This morning seven of the dark lords, along with their attendants and beasts, had thundered through the straw left standing after the harvest. Having feasted on game, the varr would be willing to amuse themselves with wilier quarry, if it offered itself.

It was a rare person who was capable of eluding the varr for a night and a day, but winning meant a life of ease for the winner and his family. Even losers sometimes survived, should they give good enough sport. Those who died were honored as forest guardians.

Two tears ran down Aubry's cheeks. Wiping his face with the back of his wrist, the man went on watching, knowing, though they did not look, the unmen watched him back. Feeling their will on him, he shuddered. Just a moment, two, more and he would walk forward.

❏❐

The banging on the front door made Gerlac jerk awake, weapon in hand. He stood, head tilted, listening to the murmur of biologics. Inhabited, the lodge was setting itself in order. Already the air had the green smell that meant it had been filtered.

A chuckle of water from what had been a dripping spigot showed that the pump muscles were back up to strength. Turning the stream off, one-handed, the black-and-white went on scouting as the thumping downstairs continued. *Keep it up*, the soldier thought, *I want to know how long it takes to trip the defenses.*

Terror oozed through his guts when he saw Ayana and the kit were not in the one room the woman had arranged to her satisfaction before she collapsed. He found her asleep in a chair in the next, one naked breast half-exposed under tumbled hair.

The kit was curled on her thighs, silent, alert. The noise had awakened it, too.

"Broo," said Gerlac softly to it, and went warily downstairs.

"Ahh!" shrieked someone and the pounding stopped. The guards captain smiled grimly. Not bad, considering the lodge was awaking from dormancy. It would get much faster as it became sure of its inhabitants.

The welt-streaked servant on the other side of the door looked about the way the soldier felt. The man eyed the pellet projector in the black-and-white's hand, and said, "You're to come to the communications center immediately."

Gerlac grunted and made the servant stand well away while he resealed the door. It was an insult, but he intended to start as he meant to continue. They walked up the stone-flagged path in ill-tempered silence, except for the inquisitive rustle of leaves.

The planetary governor was, "—distressed that Ayana was taking employment of any kind, particularly work so menial, and so soon after the death of her husband and child. The newly widowed daughter of his old friend—"

Gerlac let the words wash over him.

"—after all, hardly a day ago," continued the official. "It is, of course, your decision to make—"

When the governor ran silent, the soldier said, "I have the authority of the Red Lord. The lady will receive every consideration."

The official's mouth fell open, then closed to a disciplined line. His entire family had served, or was serving, or hoped to serve, the varr, and the dark lords exacted obedience. "Yes," he said. "Thank you."

Gerlac made a meaningless obeisance, and cut the circuit. Watching the cloak of the dancer that was the stand-by logo turn from day to night, the black-and-white said, "Naan," to himself. *The Lord of Yost has chosen.*

◻◻

Human farming depends on controlling crops and their environment. The dark lords, masters of biological systems, design ecologies to produce the cultivars they prefer across whole landmasses, seas, even planets. Yost is a varr world.

On its great plains, the wind lifts the germinals from the tassels and broadcasts them to be eaten by grain-moles. The undigested seed in the tunnel-castings sends taproots deep into the drying soil. On Yost's high plains, autumn is drought; winter, rain; spring, growth; and summer's end is harvest.

Self-seeding crops find their own microclimate, so satellites map the patches of grain for the harvest pilots. The starchy tassels are screened and cleaned as they are sucked through the bore to the geostationary orbital ports where the freighters are loaded.

From the Introduction to The Histories of Kendre Kant.

◻◻

Gerlac put down his carving as Yvandre ran by, naked as the day he was decanted. *Looks like Ayana lost the first round in the battle of the bath.* The black-and-white wiped his knife, thoughtfully, then changed his mind and drew the sharp edge carefully down the wood.

It was a warm day, cloudy. Let the kit have his little victory.

"Yvandre!" wailed a distant voice.

The soldier smiled. He could have ordered anything he wanted for the pyrrin, but he had his reasons for patiently carving the not-yet-needed weight-stick. The kit would not have the adult years Gerlac had spent, learning traditions as well as strength and skill.

"Yvandre!" Ayana was getting farther away.

The guards captain listened to woman's voice fade and smiled. She hadn't seen which way the kit had gone. "Yvandre?" he said conversationally. *Just because I didn't look at you didn't mean I didn't see you*, he thought. *A valuable lesson, in itself.* "Come here."

Tassels flared, the kit eased itself out of the thorn-bushes, filthy from bits and pieces of the leaves he'd crouched among, but unscratched by the vicious barbs. Gerlac nodded at the door. "Go let Ayana clean you up."

"Sst," it said and jogged off, having lost fairly.

Gerlac smoothed the wood, fingers feeling for what his natural eye couldn't see. It was an amiable little brat, and he was looking forward to its starting to talk. Three or four more years, they thought. Maybe five. There was some variability.

Yvandre's nominal sire, Yesdar, might have given a better estimate, but the old planetary lord, who had chosen to clone an older strain of its type rather than itself, was dead, and the precipitate breakup of its household had not been conducive to the preservation of personal files.

The fire probably was an accident, rather than the result of policy, but it had been convenient for factions other than Yesdar's own. Beltar's investigation of the matter had been cursory: the human staff had understood the Red Lord did not want answers.

There had been rumors that Beltar did not need to ask questions, but Gerlac discounted that. If the Red Lord had not gotten the kit out of the way, Yvandre would be dead. Still, duty-bound though it was to preserve the only living example of Yesdar's type, Beltar's good will was not to be counted on.

The guards captain sighted down the length of wood. *This stick would do, for the moment, but if he could get some real—*

"Where have you been? Look at you!"

Gerlac sheathed his knife and went to negotiate a settlement.

❑❐

The high blue skies of summer turned to the silver glare of autumn. Lashed by dry lightening, the sea of harvest-tousled straw burst into flame, and the smell of burning spread across the continent.

Restless, the herds and packs waited in ash-powdered forests in river valleys, sniffing the wind. When the winter rains began, the trails and trods up to the high plain were churned to mud in the rush toward fresh pastures.

By the time the new shoots were knee-high, hunted and hunters were in the thick grasses that bound the dunes and sand bars of the eastern shore. There they would birth foals and kits to follow them west through the sea of green grain.

The po-bird sang in the pana tree, and it was summer again.

❏❐

It is like rising from the bottom of a pool, thought Gerlac, *reaching for that shimmering where water yields to air.* The dark filled the depths of the valley; the air above was bright with starlight. A beautiful night that he would have preferred to spend in bed.

The whisper of waterfalls came and went on a fitful wind that smelled of jungle growth and dissolution. Every person at Varrdunost who could walk, and a few who could not, was on the ancient stairs to the plain. Some, eager to see the arrival one more time, rode on the shoulders of their kin; others, carried in a parent's arms, were about to see their first.

Although Yvandre was climbing up, Gerlac expected to carry it down. The kit's long-toed feet, deft and flexible, were not designed for extensive walking. On-world, by preference, varr rode or were carried almost everywhere they had to go outside their quarters. Designed for deep space, they were at a disadvantage in a gravity well.

When the climbers topped the cliff, everyone spread out, facing the paler sky in the east. Gerlac put one hand on Yvandre's shoulder to make sure his charge didn't stray, and gave Ayana an annoyed glance she did not see. She was the one who insisted they come with the rest.

They all stood, waiting, as the stars winked out. The soldier was impatient. A link would tell them how close the harvest crew was to bringing the bore into position in plenty of time to get the ground crew in place, let alone spectators. Instead, dressed in their best, everyone came here and watched.

"Ha-ah," called a male voice on two notes. Ayana leaned down, whispered something to the kit, and the titular Lord of Yost was gone, running east into the grain. Surprised, Gerlac saw Ayana was shivering with emotion. "Hey-ay," came the voice again.

A ragged male chorus, voices rich with conviction, sang wordlessly, or in some language that the guards captain had never heard, as the eastern clouds flushed coral. It was a harvest day, dry and windless, the kind his father—

Gerlac felt cool morning air fill his open mouth.

There was a thread of fire across the sky. Following the leading edge of daylight for guidance to the local terrain, the end of the oncoming skyhook rose out of the fiery glow of the rising sun. The blue glow of the jets told the black-and-white, to his relief, that it was being steered.

He closed his mouth. As those around him sank to the ground, it seemed quite natural to fall to his knees, too, if not in holy terror, then in awe. The soldier drove his fingers deep into the soil with the rest of them, to keep the world from spinning away beneath him.

At the spume of golden chaff when the bore took its first bite of the crop, the guards captain was on his feet and running, the sound of Ayana's "Gerlass!" far behind before it registered. The damn thing was beautiful. Yvandre would head right for it. He was not about to let his brat get killed.

Coursing the slot made by the running kit, the soldier breasted a low rise and saw Yvandre, suspended by the air-thrusters beyond reach. Someone in orbit was playing with the kit, for the suction was nothing like what it would be when the torrent of grain poured toward orbit.

Breath tearing in his lungs, the black-and-white sank to his haunches. *No wonder some think the varr gods*. On that thought, he staggered to his feet, sighted back along his trail. Yes, in a few moments, the kit, flying in its cloud of gold, would be visible from where Ayana and the others stood.

He heard the melancholy hoot of the huyuum-horn: sighted. Gerlac walked forward, feet barely touching the ground, singing imperatively to the sensors. It's too young for much of this—

Saw the kit lowered, wrapped it in his arms, safe from the whirlwind, then felt it lift them both in a storm of pelting chaff. His heart gave a great painful leap and began beating again. *Yvandre*, he thought, eyes closed, gripping the laughing kit, *you'll be the death of me.*

❏❐

The unman ruffed, and ruffed again, bored. Being confined while in transit was hard on all dark lords and this one had never developed any tolerance of strange humans. "A game, Pyrrin?" asked the bravest of its staff, proffering the three-layered board with its three-times sixty-four squares.

If they could distract it—

Silent, the planetary lord snapped its tassels. The man quickly absented himself. There was going to be trouble. Let the ship's captain, foolish enough to lodge a very young human notable on the same deck as a varr diplomat, deal with the results of his stupidity.

❏❐

A shower of pana fruit, accurately aimed, caught Gerlac around the head and shoulders. He stalked around the tree again, watching the leaves overhead, clod of dirt in hand. "Yvandre!" yelled the man, and threw, catching the fleshy pad of a hip a stinging blow.

The startled kit lost his grip, fell.

Gerlac caught the plunging body and sagged to his knees. Furious, Yvandre tried to bite. The man thumped the beast's back against the ground, held it still by both shoulders, and began to talk. "You," he said, "can't always have your own way—"

"Ssss," said the varr. *Can too.*

"Everyone needs rules." The kit, spoiled by all who came in contact with him, was becoming unmanageable, and worse, thoughtless of consequences. Gerlac was uncertain what to do. His father had taken a switch to him if he even talked back, but using corporal punishment on any varr was long-term suicide.

Short-term, if you were unlucky.

❏❐

The diplomat hissed and swung, tired of this human who kept trying to brush against him, to touch him. The man, too young perhaps to have much sense, laughed at the gesture, danced close again, eager to scent himself with the dark lord's musk. The unman swung once more, smelled blood, and then gave itself to the red rage.

❏❐

Gerlac stared after Ayana's retreating rear and wished he knew what to say. The kit probably did. Courtesies were unnecessary for a varr, but it would be like Ayana to tell Yvandre the proper way to proposition a lady.

Not, the soldier thought, *that propositioning is exactly what I have in mind.* He was old enough to think of heading a household and the two of them got on well together. "To hell with it," he said under his breath, then raised his voice to call, "Yvandre!"

Another practice session seemed in order. The kit needed to learn how to keep fighting when it was tired, and as for himself, he would not be able to sleep unless he was exhausted. "Yvandre!" he called again, but the kit did not come. "Shit," he said aloud for the first time in a long while. Then again, "Shit!"

❑❐

Rumor went whispering through the ship. There had been a killing. Men who had blithely thumbed release forms regretted their optimism. Women who had eyed the exotic alien shuddered and stayed in their quarters. The crew went about the necessary tasks in wary pairs.

Varrr, said all the whispering voices, varrrr are like that. The dark lord would pay the death-fee and think nothing of the incident. Trapped humanity could think of nothing else. It was common knowledge that the dark ones were mankillers, designed to prey on humans.

❑❐

The black-and-white put his hands on Yvandre's shoulders and kissed its forehead. Desperate for some way to proceed, and without guidance from the dark lords, he had begun training the kit in the only discipline he knew: soldiering.

Arrogant though it was, the young varr knew it needed military skills. It had seen other types of clones when they had come for the autumn hunt, taller, heavier, and far more fierce than it was. Gerlac's charge was not, and never would be a match for such, and yet it would have to make its way among them merely to survive.

To succeed, if would have to be better.

That was—improbable.

The soldier hoped his charge did not understand how improbable.

"Once more," Gerlac said, picking up the black sphere, "for luck. Then we'll quit for the day." Yvandre put out cupped hands and waited, vulnerable expression in high contrast to its broadening shoulders and lengthening legs. The unman would count it a near adult soon, and test it accordingly.

I have a year, thought the man. *Maybe no more, even though it looks like this type gains its size late.* There was no set age when the dark lords gathered their young adults together for the trials, yet he knew the time when the next group would be formed must be near. Every ten-days that call did not come was a gain.

The soldier thumbed on the timer.

Yvandre's near-human looks would cause it trouble with the other unmen. It needed to be quick, strong, able to endure pain, or the other young varr would mob it and none of the adults would stop them. Natural loners, varr were not kind to their own.

The sphere buzzed.

First warning.

"This time," said Gerlac, "I don't want to see any expression."

A startled glance, and Yvandre's face might have been carved.

The guards captain felt the tingle in his fingers, and dropped the sphere into the kit's hands. The pain would be agonizing in moments. The man looked away. He hated what he did, but not to do it required admitting the kit could not succeed, should enjoy its destined-to-be-short life.

Gerlac could not face that.

❑❐

The drumming had gone on for a long time. Most years someone stood up quickly, and men and women gave desultory chase before beginning the real business of the night, hunting one another through the standing straw. This year the dark lords had come and, if it were played at all, the game would be in earnest.

There was no stranger come to volunteer in the village. False dawn was lightening the sky before Liane rose. Her mother disgraced the family with one loud no before, mouth muffled, she was hurried away. Being the prey was a great honor. The offer must not be sullied by family regrets.

Taking the wood stacked ready, the young woman built her own pyre. If she were lucky, Liane would not be on it when it burned, would be one of the few who could boast they'd seen their own death-fire. Tucking the last piece in, she joined the elders and went to meet the dark ones.

❏❐

Gerlac swung vigorously, left a long streak of red down the kit's bare leg. "Not fast enough," he said. His student peered back at the mark and returned to the ground. "Remember the right foot." The kit nodded, began its run and leap again.

This time it got away.

The black-and-white nodded with grim satisfaction.

It was quick. He'd trained it to be, because it was never going to win any fight on reach and bulk. Yvandre's best weapons were its brains and well-trained body, and no matter how good it was would still be in mortal danger from the other, more massive, types of varr.

The soldier called his pupil down and moved on to new ground. "Show me how you'd get from here," the man pointed, "to there," he pointed again, "without being heard."

The kit moved slowly over a projected route. Gerlac kicked a convenient stone out of the way.

"Again." The soldier broke down an overhanging branch. "Again." Finally the kit sank on its haunches, shook his head. "If you have to?" Yvandre slid to its feet, flashed across the leafy clearing, dropped, rolled, this way, that, and was hidden by the boulder on the far side.

The man laughed and holstered his projector. "Let's see you."

The soft inky pellet had splashed red across one buttock, but the soldier judged it only a flesh wound, not crippling. "Better," he said, then, "Sponge that off." Ayana would have a fit if the kit showed up looking bloodied. He worked it nude so that its clothes would stay clean and cover most of the inevitable bruises.

He tapped another magazine into the projector. They made the pellets in colors other than red, but Gerlac had seen men freeze when they discovered their own, real, blood was not blue or green. It paid not to have an instant's hesitation. Combat was won and lost on just such differences.

Tomorrow he would use the ones with pain-additive, reproduce the shock of being wounded. Gerlac sighed and wiped his face. There was so little time, and so much to teach. The kit stood, alert, tassels fanned. "Ready?" said the soldier, and fired without waiting for a reply. War was, by definition, unfair.

❑❐

The man pressed his mud-streaked body in among the grassroots and froze, pricked on the back. Rolling over, he stared into pitiless gray eyes. *I gave you two days' good sport*, thought Kenson, his mouth too dry to beg. *Two days. That should be enough.*

The dark lord leaned onto its lance.

Pinned to the ground, the man writhed and died.

The unman touched, licked the bloody tips of its talons reflectively, remembering other days, other places. Local custom must be observed. That rule was quite inflexible. Here humans did not expect the prey to be eaten.

Still, the memories the taste brought were pleasant: sunlit days and moonlit nights, riding, head lifted, the scent of terror growing stronger and stronger with every beast-stride. It had seen some fine hunting in its time and would again.

Meanwhile, with an eye out for its fellows, the varr licked again.

Just a taste more—

There was no disgrace in being tempted.

❑❐

It was late, and the kit had long since been sent to bed. Ayana folded away whatever thing she had been using to keep her hands busy. Gerlac gave a final loving rub to his carving as she walked across the room. "Sleep well," she said.

He looked at her, turned sideways in the door-way, and longed.

She looked back.

The farmer's son rose, careful not to move too fast, as if the lady were a wild creature that would run and hide from him. Putting a hand on her shoulder, he said, "Ayana?"

She didn't pull away.

He embraced her, and she responded, both cautious at first, then all eager hands, and mouths, and skin on skin, until they lay, mostly nude, on the rug by the fire, her fingers twisted into his chest hair so that it stung, just a bit.

She was, he thought, *so lovely with the firelight on her*. He pressed his lips to a bare shoulder. *Ayana is always very beautiful*. Closing his eyes he brushed her face with his lips, tasted her with his tongue.

"Gerlass?" she said.

He smiled. The lady never had learned how to pronounce his name. "Umm?" he answered.

❑❐

The drummer stopped, hearing riders coming down the path from the highlands. The varr drew rein at the edge of the shadows that encircled the watch fire. One servant rode forward, leading a pack animal. Men ran to lift it onto the pyre the man himself had built two days ago.

With hasty care, women washed away paint and mud, and covered the staring face with a mask of scarlet po-bird feathers after anointing its eyes, ears, tongue, and nose. It was less than they ordinarily would have done, but it was unwise to irritate the dark lords with lengthy ritual.

The varr sat on their snake-necked mounts, showing they were alive only by the glint of a gray eye or the shift of a white hand on the reins. Oil poured, and all set ready, Cam went to the varr closest to the cross-stacked wood and bowed.

It drew and fired.

The pyre erupted into flame, illuminating the dark lords' alien faces. There were seven and three among them were exactly alike. A young clone triple, on their first hunt, perhaps, each eager to outdo the others. Had they been less competitive the man might not have died.

When the seven dark ones lifted their reins and rode away, Cam, the oldest one among villagers, came forward and kissed the ground where the unmen had waited. The wind in the trees, the voice of the spirits, sighed, accepting their gift. That done, the drummers began again, a different beat.

They had been blessed and it was time to rejoice.

❑❐

The light behind the shutters was sunrise red, and it was more than time he get up and go to his own bed. Yvandre woke early. Gerlac tugged his pants up—his shirt hadn't made it upstairs—opened the door and slid through, intent on not waking Ayana—

And was struck with a tremendous blow on his head and shoulders. Standing, dazed and barefoot, it was a few moments before his startled nose told him he was covered with fresh hartebuck dung.

It had been packed in a sack of woven green leaves that had fallen apart on impact. He poked about. The trap had not been rigged to catch the first person through. Yvandre had waited in the shadows to make sure of his victim.

Having brushed as much off as possible, Gerlac got a pail and shovel and went at the mess methodically. He was silently reminiscing about mornings as a boy, mucking out stables, when Ayana opened the door, gasped at the stench, and gaped at him.

"Stay in there until I get this cleaned up."

"What happened?" she asked from behind the closed door.

"Yvandre," said Gerlac, carefully scraping the floor-stones clean. The household biologics could only handle so much so fast and he could hardly get filthier.

"Gerlass?"

"Yvandre," he said more loudly.

"Ah," she said, and the man, hearing a hint of satisfaction, reflected she would be less pleased if she understood that Yvandre's jealousy was likely to be more straightforward than filial. Varr expected to be indulged. Gerlac had hoped the kit would be older before this problem arose.

Actually, what he'd hoped was that the kit would develop other interests first. Still, he didn't regret the night. Releasing the scrubbers to finish the work, he smiled as he carried his stinking load down into the yard, where it could do the pana some good.

"Naan," he said, thoughtfully, as he tipped up the bucket. As his father would have said, his stubborn was up. It would do the Lord of Yost no harm to learn something about human beings. "Yvandre?" he called to the world at large, "I want to speak to you."

❑❐

The woman had become one of the dead when she slipped into the tall grass, prey for the dark lords. Out of sight, and in the night, there had been tears, but no one raised the mourning wail at dawn. Those who grieved did so in silence and in shame.

A good death, everyone said publicly. The new spirit-guide, fresh from the living and knowing the people and ways of its home, would benefit them all. In a world so full of hazards, one of their number was, after all, a small price to pay for the benefits of varr rule.

❑❐

Gerlac had washed himself under the yard tap before he began searching. Given the delay, he didn't expect immediate success, but now the sun was well past its zenith, and he was re-examining territory he had already been over. The kit was clever, but it couldn't fly, there would be signs—

If he could find them.

It was a long time since Yvandre had been required to come when called. A person with a pellet-projector held to the base of his skull is unreliable, and the soldier did not want it possible for an enemy to force Ayana or someone else to call the kit and then take it.

Right now this precaution was a nuisance.

"Yvandre," the soldier yelled again, knowing he was advertising his frustration to a waiting set of ears. Gerlac was reasonably sure his charge had taken to the trees. When the kit was younger, the trunk of the pana had had clawed bark from its unauthorized nighttime roaming.

"'vandre!" The man's voice echoed back off the rocks at the stream.

Now, of course, the beast knew better than to leave such obvious traces.

The soldier sighed and sat down, resigned. The damn brat was probably watching him, was certainly listening, and had no intention of coming in until his guardian lost his temper. The black-and-white was tempted to just go home.

Where he would have to face a frantic Ayana, who was convinced that the kit needed food at regular intervals and that sleeping in a bed was essential to good health. The black-and-white knew better, but was in no mood to argue with the woman. Someday she might be right to worry.

The varr might have broken its fool neck.

Something pattered down around Gerlac, and it wasn't rain. He stood up and whirled the weighted line he'd carried hidden in his hand. The selected branch shook violently, then slowly bowed toward the ground. Yvandre slid out from among the leaves, feet first, naked except for his knife belt, ready for a fight.

Which Gerlac had no intention of giving him.

"Well," said the urine-dappled soldier, "what have you got to say for yourself?" Nothing, of course, since Yvandre, lavish with noises, still didn't use spoken language. Mopping his neck, Gerlac looked forward to the day when they could just yell and scream at one another.

"Phfitt," said the varr.

The man ignored the contempt and began to talk.

If Ayana was naive about the kit, Gerlac was not. Barracks-talk had been a quick education in the habits of the unmen. Young varr became interested in sex early; many of their female caretakers were obliging. Yvandre must be cautioned not to shock Ayana, and she must be convinced not to flirt with it.

Gerlac moped again, and began, "Ayana—"

The varr yawned, allowing its fangs to slot into place.

It was an implicit threat.

The black-and-white had come to understand Beltar's choice of him on that doom-dark sunny morning years ago: a man needed to be a battle-hardened soldier in order to survive raising a young varr. "Now, you listen to me—" he said, tempted to use corporal punishment and knowing much better than to try.

❏❐

They raked the ashes out and built a cairn of cobbles brought from the riverbank. Next hunting season, when the place was overrun by new greenery, the villagers would come to ask the guardian to turn away the ruff-cat and hurry on the harte-buck, then free the woman's spirit to roam the forest. After that ceremony no one would name the dead again.

❏❐

Both basically clean after the swim, nonetheless man and varr set their clothes to soak and washed again under the tap in the yard. Hair wet, and in stiff, fresh pants and shirts, the delinquent pair sat at the table and watched the shadows of tree leaves flicker on the floor in absolute silence.

The meal was placed on the table with a tight-lipped quietness Gerlac remembered from childhood. His mother had known how to say a great deal by saying nothing.

Yvandre, quick up the uptake, glanced from the female human face to the male and then studied its plate as the lady sat down.

The overdone roast fell in ragged slices that crumbled at the touch of Gerlac's fork. The knife squeaked on the platter as he put it down. The meat was tasteless for the man, like ashes for the varr, but both ate stoically.

Hands plaited under her chin, Ayana watched and said nothing.

Clearing his plate resolutely, the black-and-white considered his options. Today's little adventure was a storm that would have passed before the sun rose tomorrow. But there was a real, underlying problem. Yvandre's drive for dominance must be sublimated.

Occasionally.

Gerlac took another gray slice, spooned gravy over it. He was going to have to separate Yvandre from servants who put too many ideas about in their young lord's head and away from villagers in whose eyes the young varr could do no wrong.

The soldier cut and chewed.

Yvandre's gaining discipline was not a matter of convenience. Its sire, Yesdar, had been a diplomat working in human space, a profession necessary to, but not necessarily respected among, the varr. The guards captain hoped for better for his charge.

It it survived.

Ayana thumped a casserole of fruit onto the table, and the two males looked sideways at one another. Gerlac served himself, said, "Looks good," into the silence. Yvandre, not fond of sweets, wielded the serving spoon delicately, knowing a polite guest must eat almost anything that isn't poisonous.

That much diplomacy the black-and-white could teach.

☐☐

She came, dropping between night and dawn, the time when the eyes are easily deceived because the mind is tired or not yet fully awake. Thumping into the grasslands, Constance wriggled out of her protective harness, tapped open the hatch, and was out and into cover.

Enzymes activated by her absence, the pod was already slumping into an amorphous goo. Her safety depended on moving as quickly and as silently as possible away from it and the line of descent the varr's ever-watchful surveillance would have traced. They might note so large a meteor for investigation.

Panting, she zigzagged on, trying to leave as little trail as possible. Stealth was her only real weapon against the dark lords' security. Once they knew they needed to look, they would find her. Guaranteed. *I'm not here*, Constance thought, as if someone could hear her thoughts. *Not here.*

Although she had chosen to shelter in a forest where humans came and went regularly, it would take the greatest care to survive the plants long enough to begin the next stage of her plan: joining a village near the dark lords' hunting grounds.

❑❐

Gerlac reached up, broke a branch, started to strip the leaves, and stopped. He tossed his first selection aside, and cut a slim, leafy wand. He might win the skirmish with a few stout whacks to the buttocks, but he was more likely to win the war with a light blow to the pride.

If he could contrive one.

The soldier switched his hand and it stung, a little. It was probably good that Ayana preferred a courtly battle of wits, but the young varr's guardian was not pleased that arguments could be shifted onto ground where he was at a loss. He twitched the switch.

Women.

For that matter, varr.

Lucky the kit still hasn't learned how to talk, thought the man, grimly. He would not bet on Ayana when Yvandre got his tongue. The kit was clever. Gerlac grinned, looking forward to hearing the pair square off against one another. Varr-like, his charge was not willing to lose at anything.

The soldier tossed the switch away.

It had been a stupid thought.

❑❒

Something avian was watching her, and Constance could not tell if it was natural curiosity, or something infinitely more dangerous, a watcher. The varr crafted living flesh as men worked clay. That bird-brain might not be that of a bird.

On the other hand, she was tired and hungry, and knew it would not take much to alarm her. Ignorant, Constance had to learn enough about the forest to pass as a stranger looking for a new village when the locals found her, as they would, eventually.

Wit, wit, wit, sang the creature.

❑❒

Bare bellies, breasts and buttocks sun-dappled, twenty people crossed the courtyard and vanished into the jungle. Gerlac avoided catching anyone's eye. He'd stared the first time he saw the naked procession, and the gatherers had not missed a chance since to discomfit him.

Last time, one woman had wagged everything she had at him, while the others fell about laughing. Frowning, the guards captain keyed himself into the still-sleeping main house, alert for anything unusual, although his thoughts followed the gatherers into the maze of green.

They were the ones who gathered the bales of leaves and bark, the bags of dried insects, and the carboys of liquid that filled the front hall. Almost half the income of Varrdunost came from deep jungle. The highlands' grain was not nearly as valuable by weight, and since the crop was self-sowing, the estate manager—

He did not want to think about his problem.

If, the guards captain added to himself that was what one could call it.

His time with Yvandre was drawing to a close. Gerlac lived from moment to moment as he had when in active combat, refusing to waste himself on the nonessential, driving both the kit and him-self in an effort to prepare it to compete against its age-mates.

It was not going to be enough.

Yvandre did not mass enough, was too docile, was—

At least it would die quickly.

I'm a soldier, reflected Gerlac, as he turned on the communications equipment. *I'll just move on.* Thinking about Ayana, he jabbed a button harder than was necessary, stubbed his finger, and cursed. Soldiers who put down roots were fools. He pressed his hand to his eyes.

And took it away as Yvandre came in, chewing something from the kitchen. The kit ate constantly and still looked too lean for his frame. Gerlac emphatically tweaked another setting. Slow to mature, this growth spurt had left the young varr struggling to control its changing body, clumsy.

Clumsy could be fatal, if there were only a few more months. That was not enough time for its natural grace to reassert itself. The kit wandered out again, probably on its way back to the kitchen. The soldier opened his mouth to call it back, then let it go. Food might do it more good than another session with the security systems.

Certainly he didn't feel like arguing about it. Gerlac checked the monitors to the rooftop where the freight dirigibles waited, half-inflated, in their cradles. They would not be sailing today: the wind was against them. Popping satellite views in and out, he queried the network of AIs, checked the logs.

Varrdunost had an excellent passive system that the black-and-white didn't trust. Breaking such defenses was his own specialty. Anything automated could be fooled. There was no substitute for going out, walking around, smelling and tasting, running the soil through one's fingers.

Gerlac began noting locations that should be inspected. One meteor in particular struck him as suspicious. There had not been a flash when it hit. Anything that made a soft landing could have a passenger. There was no legitimate reason to sneak onto Yost—

The unexpected message came in as he was about to close things done for the morning. If the kit passed several trials of the Red Lord's choosing, then there would be no need for Yvandre to undergo the first round of competition with its age-fellows.

The soldier printed it out, read it again.

It was a reprieve from near-certain death.

The Red Lord must have other, unsuspected, informers on the household staff and an unsuspected willingness to protect Yesdar's heir. Gerlac tapped the flimsy against his palm, thinking.

This—variance—made it likely that Beltar intended the kit for a diplomatic position, where its ability to fight, or even to socialize with its fellows in the normal manner, would be of minimal importance. Yvandre's working lifetime was likely to be short and unpleasant.

Sighing, the soldier admitted to himself that he'd known all along. Yesdar's death years in the past, there was no other reason to keep the kit in total isolation from its kind. He had hoped it was neglect, the press of other business, something like that—

But Beltar was reputed to neglect nothing. Gerlac checked the system settings again, closed the door, and bipped his list to locate the kit. Out of the building already, on his way home. *It's getting altogether too casual about getting permissions,* he thought. *Time for a bit more discipline.*

Stepping through the open door of the lodge into the savory fug of Ayana's cooking, he called, "Yvandre?" The hungry kit would not have roamed far. "Yvandre." The white face, framed by the black tassels, materialized in the gloom at the top of the stairs.

Gerlac gestured. Since the varr did not speak, he and Ayana had fallen into using a sketchy version of the gestures the military used in silent communication. One-handed, Yvandre said, wait a moment, and vanished on some last-moment business of its own.

The man dreaded its going beneath the Three.

At least it was not certain death, as the alternative was. Rubbing the scar on his face, the guards captain remembered of one of the older men telling a green farm boy that, for a soldier, any day you weren't dead was a good day. "What's for first meal?" he called.

"What did you let him eat?" rebutted Ayana from the kitchen.

Coming in, Gerlac spread his hands in negation, said, "Nothing."

The sound she made was exceedingly unladylike.

"I didn't let him eat anything," the soldier said, helping himself to a slice of pana and eluding a smart hand slap. "The kitchen staff fed him."

Ayana expressed silent contempt for this bit of casuistry.

"He's bottomless, anyway," added Gerlac. "Read this."

Wiping her hands, she took the printout. Ayana's face brightened and she hugged the soldier. One hand sticky, he put an arm around her, grinned. "Safe," she said softly. "It honors some old statues and that's it?"

"You read the message," said Gerlac, and kept his thoughts and his reasoning to himself. The guards captain hoped no one told her about the Three. As to whether any of what he had been told was true, he would be finding out, soon enough. "Yvandre?" the soldier called. "First meal!"

Without a sound on the stair, it stood in the door.

❑❐

Wit, wit, wit! Wherever Constance went, a bird was there, persistent and out of sight. It was unnatural that species live in so many different types of habitat. She had retreated into the deeper woods, hoping there, at least, they would not alert human beings to her presence.

The problem was that in the older forest, where trees had fallen and left the ground open to the sky, the undergrowth clawed at you, and not just metaphorically. The plants seemed to crave blood. She had to keep peeling sharp-toothed suckers from her legs and unwinding barbed vines from her neck and face.

Only at night, if she found a clear place, could Constance look up and see what direction she had moved in. It had been several days since a break in the canopy of green. The ground beneath her feet was sloping, ever so gently down, and she was afraid she was approaching Ootorono.

The lake had an evil reputation.

❏❐

To take advantage of Beltar's gift of time, Gerlac skipped several stages. Yvandre was quick and clever, better to build on that as quickly as possible. The varrling needed to learn how to survive long enough to learn in a strange environment.

The forest would do, for a start, although the ultimate problem was the compound where the young varr strove against one another until half were dead or permanently crippled. A state as good as being dead, given the varr gave no medical aid to incurables.

They were kinder to their human soldiers than to themselves. He'd seen them stand and watch one of their own bleed out when a physician said an injury would not heal completely. The victim had accepted the death sentence as silently as its impassive fellows.

Varr could not accept themselves as less than perfect.

Gerlac reset his eye, and checked his surroundings. He'd hoped for an earlier start, but the departure of the expedition had been postponed by Ayana's loud and indignant discovery of live hartebuck calf in the pantry.

The kit was silly with glee, and the soldier had to smother reluctant pride. It had taken real skill to capture the beast unharmed and bring it into the house without being seen, for the calf weighed as much as Yvandre. It was the sort of stunt that would win respect from other young varr.

The problem was that when Ayana untied the calf, it kicked her, and then ran, wild-eyed, through the clean laundry on dung-fouled hooves. Watching the beast clear the wall, bonneted with one of his shirts, Gerlac strangled his laughter, told the kit to apologize, and volunteered to hang the rewashed clothes.

She had gathered the lot up and stomped off. The woman could have the whole job done up at the main house for no more than the trouble of telling someone to come and pick it up, but Ayana did everything by herself. Whatever, the silly incident had forced a day's delay in the soldier's plans.

Pinning wet cloth, Gerlac brooded on why the ex-governor's daughter wanted to act like some farmwoman, then went on to why a security expert, getting too old for his rank, was playing nursemaid, and was well on his way to a black rage fueled by anxiety when he pinned the last cloth to the line.

Tucking the empty basket under his arm, Gerlac went to walk the short perimeter trail. He hoped to find his missing shirt and his temper. By the time he got back, everything would be dry, ready to be taken to Ayana for smoothing, folding, and putting away. Tomorrow he and Yvandre would go to the Three.

One more day before the kit entered the tombs beneath the ancient statues, and Gerlac hardly knew what to do with himself. He'd briefed Yvandre, which was why the uncharacteristic foolishness, and had not told Ayana what they would be doing was dangerous.

She knew, or had found out, anyway.

Basket hanging at his side, the man watched a lizard skim from tree to tree, snap once in midair and land with its mouth ruffled by deflating wings. One movement of the jaws, two, and the gaily frilled symbiont was gone.

The guards captain whacked the tree-trunk with his basket and watched the lizard sail away. He was a realist. Mature, Yvandre would be in constant peril, but the varr's wanton waste of their own sickened him. Perfection had too high a price.

Gerlac whacked the basket against another tree trunk and was pelted with overripe pana fruit. He cursed fervently. Now he would have to wash himself and the basket. "—to the seventh generation," he concluded, and stopped, sniffing.

Rotting flesh. Tucking his basket into a convenient crotch, the black-and-white drew his weapon, and followed his insulted nose upslope. Noticing the shredded remains of his shirt waving from a bush, he thought, *Better not bring that back.*

Whatever had died was wedged under a windfall so recent the leaves were still green. The soldier heaved the fallen branches away, broke a stout stick. The carcass was of a ruff-cat, paws burned, tongue ragged. It looked like the beast had stepped in something poisonous.

But what?

And where?

And most important, why?

I can't delay the test, thought Gerlac.

❑❒

Her pursuers had spread out in a line to make sure of their prey. Wit, wit, wit! went her constant companion. In a flutter of wings it was joined by two others of its kind. Wit, wit, wit! they twittered. Pressing herself against the leafy debris of the forest floor, she heard, not too far away, human laughter.

❑❒

Gerlac did not know much about monuments and carvings, but what he did know told him the Three were ancient. Only the oldest portrayals of the varr were so informal. Heads brushed by green

leaves, robes splotched with lichen, the stone figures were four times his own height.

They were having a drinking bout.

The dozing figure on the right held a wine-cup
in one hand, carelessly tilted over. The other two,
their cups upside-down to show they were empty,
smiled at the sleeper, eyes over-wise. All three had
their headdresses pushed back from foreheads that
were going to ache in the morning.

The soldier patted one great stone toe, sympa-
thetically.

The dark lords had not always been so grim.
This had been a great pleasance when the Three
were put in place at the dawn of the world, and you
could still find black-and-white paving, as smooth
and unheaved as the day it was laid, if you scuffed
away the leaf mold.

Yvandre gave one glance to the monumental
carved faces, not so very different from its own,
and resumed watching the living forest, thinking,
perhaps that might threaten it but these stone figures could not. The black-and-white feared it was
wrong.

Still, Yesdar had chosen an older type for its
heir. Whatever guarded the tombs of Yost's earli-
est pyrrin, constructed when the varr were in the
first flush of their power, might be subtle enough
to know Yvandre for what he was. The oldest had
not lived in simple times.

The deeps were entered by a ramp of earth and vegetation that had once been steps. Somewhere below the vaults might be as they were when they were cut from the bedrock, but their opening was smothered with ancient death until it might almost have been taken for a natural hole.

Peering into the dark pit, Gerlac restrained Yvandre with a hand on his arm. "When you run out of rope, that's it." The black-and-white held up two ends and looped one into his own belt, then added, wisely, "For this time." If it was the kit's one and only chance it would be more tempted to disobey.

Yvandre nodded.

"One tug if you need me; two if you're coming out." The man tied the rope on and the varr started down. When it was out of sight, Gerlac loosened his knife in its sheath, and picked a suitable anchor point. He would cut and tie the cord if he needed to go in.

After checking the hidden weapon he was not supposed to be carrying, he settled down to wait. Beltar's priorities were not his own, and Gerlac saw no reason to honor them when he could not be observed. The object of the exercise was, after all, to produce a long-overdue replacement for Yesdar, not a corpse.

Presently the rope grew taunt, and the soldier tense with attention. Sunlight shifted silently over the forest floor. At the two-tug signal, Gerlac took a deep breath of relief. He did not fear going underground, he'd done his share of caving as a boy, but the deeps beneath the Three were not a place for any man, no matter how loyal to the varr.

No human had ever come out.

Wide-eyed, Yvandre emerged, carrying a cup. Gerlac wondered which Lord of Yost the platinum-and-ruby drinking bowl had been crafted for, and what had given it to his kit. Taking it, he saw its inside was damp. With wine, he hoped. There were other possibilities.

He turned it over. A red drop splattered at his feet, but the young varr didn't see. Its precise, focused stare was on the depths from which it had come. Even to human vision, there was a flicker of might-have-been motion in the darkness. The soldier's skin crawled.

Gerlac put a hand on the varrling: it was quivering, strung to the highest pitch. The soldier suppressed the urge to pick his kit up and run as fast as he could as far as he could. Yvandre was much too heavy, and as long as it was calm, the young varr was safe, and he was, too, as its companion.

Stripping off his shirt and wrapping the cup, the soldier breathed, "Let's go." It was getting late; Ayana would be anxious. *But not*, he thought, *as anxious as she should be.* Gerlac had not told her where they were going, or why. In that, if in nothing else, he had obeyed the Red Lord.

This was only the first test.

There would be others.

❏❐

The pursuit had encircled her with sound, wanting her to know they were there, but did nothing. *Waiting*, she thought. *For what? One of the dark lords?* Although she had intended become prey to ambush an unman, she had intended to take the varr and not the other way around.

Wit, wit, wit, said a chorus of little voices. *Nitwit is more like it*, she thought, wriggling deeper into the thicket and trying not to think about what might be about to happen to her. Intent on hiding herself, she never heard the arrow that pierced her throat.

Constance gargled blood, and died.

❏❐

Lying on his back sunbathing, the sea-beast's photosynthetic green was shaded only by the blue and violet tattoo positioned where minimal clothing would conceal it. Leaving everything that would ordinarily be seen unmarked was a discreet way of proclaiming Arl's status: he represented his clade of chimera before the Red Lord.

Not that sea-beast's design was less boastful of his ability to endure pain than most chimera's all-over body patterns. Gerlac's genitals shrived every time he saw the snake at Arl's groin, created with needles, pigment, patience, and nothing else.

Squatting, the guards captain relaxed. He was trying to recapture the habits of active service, where one took advantage of every moment of rest. He might soon be up for reassignment, if the kit died. If the kit succeeded, it would take a little longer. As for Ayana—

He sighed.

"What," the chimera asked, opening gold-green eyes.

"The Red Lord wants Yvandre to take a long swim. Alone."

Arl opened and closed his protective nose flaps, said, "Yes," in his soft voice. Varr were expected to know the capacities of those who served them. That Yvandre be required to spend time in the sea was reasonable. The chimera frowned. Rising on one elbow, he checked the man's expression and settled back. "Alone," said the sea-prince. "A test. Is it to know?"

Gerlac shook his head.

Crafted by the dark lords to serve, still the chimera thought for themselves. There had been times, in the past, when they had been outright defiant. Arl's expression said he did not approve of putting the kit at the mercy of forces of nature. "Precautions," the chimera suggested, eyes closed.

"Forbidden," said the soldier.

The sea-prince puffed air between its lips, a silent, I-dare-if-you-do.

"Yes," answered Gerlac. "How?"

Heads together, each grimacing at the other's alien breath, they began to plan.

❏❐

The guardsman scuffed the bare soil. This flat oval, where vegetation had withered to sterile ground, was not a meteor strike. Last night's rain had washed away most traces, but it was obvious that not too long ago someone had landed here and destroyed a one-time-use pod.

They were going to have to hunt for whoever it was. "Damn," he said softly. Yolani was going to be disappointed. He hoped so, anyway. She had other friends in the barracks. Tapping his communications unit, he said, "One."

"One."

"This is Twelve. We have a live one here—"

One swore violently, in violation of protocol.

"Might as well start the drill." The thunder of guards running to man flyers would tell Yolani he was not standing her up.

Another oath, more inventive than the last.

"Sir," said Twelve, neutrally. Apparently One had also had something on his personal agenda. The guardsman checked out a patch of grass and sat down to wait. When duty called, you answered, or you would not answer ever again.

He took a swallow of warm water from his canteen, rinsed it around his mouth, swallowed. Protocol required him to wait in place unless it was likely the trail be erased. The sky was a perfect, cloudless blue. Whoever would be in cover, hiding from the surveillance satellites.

There was no hurry.

⌑⌐

The concealed sensors fell down through the layers of water, warm, cool, cooler, cold, heading for the regions the where the season never changed. Terror trickled down Gerlac's spine—

"Shucked his shorts," sub-vocalized Arl.

The man breathed again.

"Moving west," added the inhuman voice. West was the nearest land. Either by deduction or luck, Yvandre had made its first correct decision. Gerlac rubbed his scar, remembering the kit's too-composed face as it donned its gear, checked it far too carefully for a casual swim in a calm sea.

When the flyer lifted away, it didn't bother to look up.

It had known what was happening, the soldier was almost certain of that, although it was not sup-posed to have received any hint. The Red Lord might not be surprised that its order not be obeyed in spirit. In letter, Beltar would expect nothing less than perfect obedience.

If they had not told the truth, neither had he nor Arl lied.

All three of them shared an unspoken under-standing.

It would be easy for things to go wrong.

❏❐

Smashing its way open-mouthed through a school of fish, the leviathan was filling its belly. Genetic programming allowed it to swim in the depths only when it needed to feed. Otherwise it floated on or close to the surface, patrolling the skies above and the seas beneath with vision and with sound, searching for anomalies.

To it, as to no natural predator, the urge to eat and the urge to hunt were disparate. Roused, it would ensac its prey and call other designed organisms to decide whether to draw human attention to the discovery. Sensing a flurry on the surface, still hungry, it began to rise.

The varr had designed it to fulfill a purpose, not to survive. If something attracted its attention it would strike, and strike again, until it had captured its prey or died. Driven by engineered need, Leviathan soared up out of the depths.

❏❐

Arl said, "Lost him. I think he's been taken." Then there was nothing but the chimera's sonic signal, here, here, here. The dot on the screen that represented the sea-beast was heading at what must be his top speed toward the fuzzy line that was the shore.

Gerlac cursed, fervently and generically, still enough in control of himself to remember that what he really wanted to say would get him court-martialed. If he were lucky. Beltar was occasionally hasty in his decisions. "I need a flyer," he said as he got to his feet, clipped an earpiece in.

"Sir."

The soldier checked his harness, listening to the chimera half-empty his lungs and grate, "Yvandre." Then, louder, "Yvandre!" Gerlac, running for the airstrip, knotted his hands into fists. The sea-beast could damage himself if he did not change over properly. The guards captain understood its desperation; he felt it himself.

"Powering up," said the pilot.

"Yvandre!" gasped the chimera in Gerlac's earpiece as he boarded. Air rasped in distended lungs. The soldier winced at the pain-filled sound. "Yvandre!" A fit of coughing, then, "I think it's landed. There's blood—"

"Ready to boost," said the pilot.

"Lift off," Gerlac snapped.

They skimmed south, the guards captain listening to the chimera hunt. "It's gone into the dunes," panted the sea-beast. From the sound, Arl had beached himself and was crawling. Webbed feet did not work well in sand.

"When we get there, bring us in fast and low," said Gerlac. Best to overfly, startle anything that was not expecting them.

"Nape of the earth," said the pilot, and complied earlier than the guards captain had intended. Gerlac avoided looking down at the wave tops fleeting beneath his feet, closer than he liked.

"Safe," said the chimera, and cut off his transmission.

That's it? Gerlac smothered resentment. Arl was correct. There might be unauthorized ears listening. They might be in race without knowing it. Yvandre was a prize without price for any poacher. "Faster," he told the pilot. "He's found it."

The man tweaked the wing-settings and wrung another modicum of speed from his craft. "Doubleharness," he said, "I'll skid it down the beach." The resulting cloud of sand would confuse any unauthorized watching eyes.

"Weapons?" said the guards captain, clipping net points.

"I have mine."

Gerlac balanced his in his hand, ready to thumb the safety off.

They came in over a mass of bleeding flesh, too large to be either varr or chimera, rolling at water's edge. Arl's work, the guards captain hoped, looking at the blood-soaked sand. But the sea-prince had said there was blood—

"Keep everything running," said Gerlac as they slid to a stop. He dropped to the beach, roared, "Arl? It's me!" Weapon in hand, the guards captain waited. It would waste time if he went to cover and they emerged. Nothing, he thought. Nothing. "Yvandre?"

They were there, of course.

Arl was just making sure.

Nonetheless, he sagged with relief when the pair appeared. "Get in," Gerlac said, then to the pilot, "Get us out." Sand spraying, the flyer rose, and arrowed over the ocean toward home, trading stealth for speed. High above them a half dozen craft swept the sky for something the guards captain hoped was not there.

❑❒

On what he thought of as the right side of the invisible boundary between varr and human space, the man lay in his ship, listening for the private signal. Constance was overdue; she was never overdue if she could help it. It was a bad sign.

Worse, it was the second rendezvous that she had not made. It began to look like she had failed. Constance's big flaw had been—was—that she got overconfident. More cautious, he might be able to succeed where she had failed. Although the stakes were too high for his taste, he would be back.

❑❒

"Yvandre!" Gerlac stared up into the foliage, wishing the kit would answer, although he couldn't complain that it didn't. The column of smoke from the landing strip did signal the kind of situation in which the kit should be cautious. "Yvandre?"

He walked forward again, taking care to show himself. Finally, a branch swept toward the ground as weight was shifted outward. The young varr dropped out of the sheltering leaves to land, upright, hands signing, What happened?

"Arl's dead," said Gerlac. "No one else was hurt."

The kit began preening its harness. The soldier started back without another word. Grief-stricken, he didn't trust himself to speak. Yvandre would not exhibit its emotions. Varr that did not conceal their thoughts did not survive.

It was a bad time to lose Arl. The kit was as spoiled for attention as Ayana could contrive. Gerlac had hoped that Arl, at once tough-minded and indulgent, could fill in for her. Quick to extrapolate consequences, Yvandre might not react well to the news of the pregnancy.

The soldier shrugged mentally. He'd thought they'd agreed to wait until Yvandre was taken from them. The governor's daughter might put the varrling ahead of her own offspring without a thought, but the farmer's son was not so blithe. Humans had instincts, too.

There were other factors. Varr competed so hard they killed their own, a human child would be nothing to their way of thinking. He didn't think Yvandre would turn on the infant, but it was possible that the something as simple as the strange scent would release hostility—

"Ayana's cooking last meal," said the soldier to the air in general.

None of them would be hungry, but making food and pretending to eat would give them something to do before the long hours of the night when they could all stare into the darkness and mourn silently. Morning, and the need to join the search for a traitor, would come soon enough.

"Yvandre?"

The varr took the lead.

The guards captain followed, rubbing his aching forehead as he went. He was near-certain the chimera's death was not an accident, had already sent for a headquarters investigative team. The sea-people had already requested the body: there was not much to give them.

Even if the investigators found nothing, the guards captain's intuition told him it was past time to retreat from this remote, ever-more-poorly defended place. Beautiful and familiar though it was, Pana Lodge was worse than useless.

"Slow down," he called to Yvandre's retreating back. The kit did not respond. "We have to stay together." The young varr paused, but it did not look back. Gerlac didn't hurry, giving it time to get its face under control.

When he came up, they embraced, hard. "I'm sorry," said Gerlac, saying what it could not say. "He was a good friend." Dangerous emotional indulgence over, man and varr walked off, each covering the trail alternately, as the drill prescribed. Before, behind, left, right, switch over—

❑◗

It was evening, the sky a blue so dark it was almost black, when the varr rode into the village. The man stumbling behind them, neck noosed and hands bound behind his back, attempted to break for the forest and was pulled off his feet with a casual tug of the rope.

The adults came out, shutting the youngsters in the houses. They knew why the dark lords had come. The penalty for sheltering a human from outside the empire was death. That they would say they did not know, would not matter. They would—and quite correctly—meet with disbelief.

They knew the penalty. If the adults submitted, their deaths would be quick and their children would live. If not, the unmen would destroy everyone and everything until it was as if this village had never been. Without meeting the unman's eyes, they sorted themselves out and lined up.

❑◗

The kit was on the flat rock by the stream, meaning it was willing to be found. Its right shoulder showed a chaff-mark, and the black-and-white gestured for the varr to unbuckle the strap, glad of the excuse. He talked better with something for his hands to do.

Yvandre wore battle-style harness, with every bit of metal blacked or covered so nothing would flash or jingle. It took steady work to keep it in good repair, and the young varr's taloned hands were not deft with tools. Threading the needle from his repair kit Geilac began overcastting the stitches at the edge of the leather.

His charge sighed and settled against him as it had when it was much younger and the world was overwhelming. The soldier pulled and looped, as the sun-motes danced in the leaves. He was in no hurry to finish the job. There would not be many more of such quiet moments together.

Ayana found them, asleep in the dappled shade, and left as silently as she had come. Hunger would bring the pair home soon enough. They were coming to a time of endings. Beginnings, too, she thought, hand on her belly, but joy would wait for sorrow.

⌐⌐

It was an inconvenience that the varrling's guardian soldier had called for official aid so promptly. Now the matter had appeared on Beltar's morning roster and security for Yost had automatically been enhanced. That would be make the problem more difficult.

Word had gone out on the far side of the border that a man would be wealthy if he arranged training accident to Yost's young varr. Something easily accepted, unsuspicious, even, in a back-handed way, resembling fair play, given the level of competition between near-adults.

Yvandre must not make it to adulthood. Its sire's constant attempts to treat with outsiders had been a nuisance. Once posted, the varrling would be difficult to destroy. It might even be successful, or at least make a beginning on Bondre's old, outdated dream. Varr had no business cooperating with feral humans.

Ours, thought the planetary lord, *is to rule. Theirs, to serve. To each what they do best.* It got to its feet in a swirl of scented robes and began to pace. Beltar was proving to be far too popular. Its own power base, though substantial, was no match. The Teyrian varr might just tip the balance.

The dark lord could not allow that. "Esth so varr," it whispered to itself. "Esth so varr." One taloned hand on the window sill, it stared into the mists of evening and saw scenes of blood and fire. They must not come again. Or if they did, it had to win. Compromise was unacceptable; defeat unthinkable.

❑❐

Gerlac looked right and left. No one would admit to knowing where Yvandre was, which meant he was with some girl, outdoors, and would not want to be disturbed. The soldier had to find his charge before its carelessness had fatal consequences. Yost was no longer safe.

The black-and-white began his stalk. Two nude figures in his sights, Gerlac considered pinging the rump of the topmost, then merely said, conversationally, "Yvandre." That he had gotten here without being noticed made his point economically.

The kit paused, furious. The soldier made an imperative gesture, then walked off. One of these days the fact that Yvandre owned the planet they stood on and everything and everyone on it would become more than an abstraction to its young lord. Then, officially or not, what little discipline Gerlac could enforce would end.

In the meantime, he had duties.

Yvandre didn't hurry, but when it appeared its clothing was in order and its harness on. Lighter, faster, and less trackable than the black-and-white, it set a pace nicely calculated to wind the older man. The soldier glared at its back, forced himself to keep up.

Damn varr, growing up too fast and not fast enough.

The soldier wondered if there were a parthenogenetic daughter or two in the nearby villages. A son, rare indeed, he would have heard of. In any case, he had been careful not to inquire. Yvandre's type was among the oldest, might have that trait in addition to the deceptively near-human face that had appealed to Yesdar, so acutely aware how appearance worked against any varr when it dealt with humans.

Gerlac picked a flower as he passed, crushed it.

He had not come looking for the varrling on a whim. The Red Lord had summoned Yvandre to him. There was no telling when or if his charge would be returning to Yost. Rumor was that the opposition to the young varr's very existence was strengthening. Diplomacy was not a well-regarded profession among the dark lords.

Looking at the back in front of him, Gerlac thought about resigning, living off Ayana's money somewhere, and worrying about nothing more difficult than raising the merely human child beginning to bulge the ex-governor's daughter's belly. *Foolishness*, he thought, and called, "Slow down."

Yvandre wasn't smiling when it looked around, but it might as well have been. Gerlac slapped it on the shoulder as he came up, but said nothing. The kit was still young enough to feel immortal. *Time for another lecture*, thought the guards captain. He took a deep breath that might almost have been a sigh.

❑❐

The package deal would have been tempting for someone with no dependents—in, kill, get out if you could—but he had been instructed to demand hostages in return for the cash up-front. Get caught, and your nearest and dearest died with you.

That gave most adventurers pause, even when they were tempted by the figures. No kin equaled no deal, and his principles expected genetic confirmation. *Still*, thought the agent, checking his list, *it will only take one. One good one, that is.*

꒰꒱

The body on the trail was headless and no threat, but its fellows could still be in the surrounding brush. Nothing moved for a long, hot time, until Gerlac turned the corpse over with his boot. The guts sloughed out, attracting his cloud of flies away from the black-and-white.

Varr kill.

The amount and location of blood showed the man had died slowly and probably painfully. It looked like the kit had discovered some of his cousins' techniques for itself. Maturing, Yvandre had become dangerous. Gerlac frowned, reflected, *I suppose that was inevitable—*

The sound made the leaves on the trees shudder. The soldier was on his belly and hidden the undergrowth without a conscious thought. It had been a human scream. Varr went silent in distress. Easing himself into better cover, the man listened.

There was nothing more.

After a while, Gerlac rose and went on. When he came to a rocky rib bare of soil and vegetation, the guards captain squatted and looked over the prospect. He'd come further than he wanted and need to stop and rethink his strategy.

Before him, the land fell away into a bowl, at whose misty heart, if the black-and-white were in his reckoning, lay Ootorono, lake of fumes and mists, an unhealthy place by all accounts. He mopped his face with his sleeve and then with repellent.

Even if none of what was rumored was true, he was in danger, unprotected by the pheromones that identified Yvandre to the deeper jungle. Gerlac took a deep breath. The wise course would be to go back. The defensible course would be to wait here. His course—

The black-and-white stood. He would follow his kit and hope he could keep himself alive until his disturbing presence in the forest drew the varrling to him. Yvandre would protect him, once it knew his guardian was here.

Trrree dee dee, coaxed something hidden in the rustling fronds of the fern-trees. Gerlac did not look up. He had covered his head by pulling his tunic up and peering through the neck-hole, but his face might prove inviting.

Aaaah sist sist sist! shrilled something deeper in.

The soldier shivered involuntarily.

The jungle was hungry.

Although Beltar had sent it in, the kit was young to be hunting on its own. Most varr striplings traveled in an uneasy, bickering pack lead by one or two of the older unmen while they learned to survive in the wild. The bottom one or two in the prestige order often didn't survive.

The rest learned to hunt, kill, and hide, from one another and other threats. Gerlac had done some preparatory work, had planned to do more, so his lighter, less aggressive charge would not be out-matched in the field. *I should have kept after it*, thought the soldier.

Beltar had sent his message directly to the varrling. Challenged, Yvandre had set out without a word to its caretakers. The guards captain could only hope that natural aptitude, identifying scent, and the unauthorized expeditions of its childhood would allow it to survive.

Eyes on the damp soil of the path, the soldier slowed, took his light from his pouch, shone it sideways to bring out the details. He knew the print. The light impression of the heel of the foot said Yvandre had been traveling at a quick, almost tip-toe, gait. Toward what?

"Awk! St! St!"

Recovering, Gerlac unfolded from his defensive crouch. Whatever that was, it was not far away, and it was possible it was what had drawn the kit's attention. All varr were curious and Yvandre was dauntingly bold besides. He remembered the kit running toward the sky hook, laughing in the uprush of air.

The man returned his weapon to his holster, made sure it was ready-to-draw. He carried it ha-bitually, although he never killed with it on his hunting expeditions, preferring to use the bow, the spear, the knife. The silent weapons had always been his choice.

The kit, with teeth and claws, had its own armament.

But varr tassels and scent glands brought a fine price in many markets in the inner cluster. Where they weren't sold openly, illicit sales brought even more fabulous prices. The black-and-white had come to warn and protect his charge. Unauthorized landings, plural, had been detected in this region.

Poachers, the soldier was sure. Surely Beltar had not envisioned such danger. The current fashion was to take the entire head and strip off the salable parts only as they were bought, thus ensuring the buyer that the goods were absolutely—

"Awk!" Weapon in hand, the soldier began moving from cover to cover, acutely conscious that the footing was treacherously soft. *If I get you out of this*, he thought, *varr or no varr, I'm going to train you so hard you'll be able to sleep standing for a month.*

The threat came neither from above or below, the two directions Gerlac most feared, but from behind, and was nothing more than a fragrance, an eddy of dizziness that drove the man to his knees. He fell flat, staring at a scribble of twisted stems that might be the last thing he—

There was a terrible pain in his chest. He was being dragged by the ankles, roughly, and without much regard for his head and shoulders. The guards captain came to himself with blue sky overhead, and thought, vaguely, *I'm being slapped.*

Yvandre snarled silently.

Well, thought Gerlac, *I'm angry too*, and parted his swollen lips to speak. The young varr put its palm over his mouth. It stared intently in the direction they both had come from. The tassels were snapped down, directing sound to its ears.

Looking where it looked, Gerlac edged to a sitting position. His stomach clenched and he swallowed bile. A unidentifiable flyer, flying a grid pattern, using grapples to uproot flora, and netting what fauna they could, hoping to hit on something profitable.

They would be eager to capture a varr. Mature dark lords were solitary hunters, and days might pass before an adult's absence became a certainty. The first and last thing the black-and-whites might learn about an abducted unman might be the location of its headless corpse.

Yvandre, and by extension, himself, were already missed or should be. Inching his way under a thin screen of leaves, Gerlac hoped Ayana forgot everything he had ever said to her about staying calm when they were late and called the main house sooner than later.

Deploying a camouflage web, the soldier knew it would not be enough, in broad daylight and on territory that the poachers might already have mapped, to completely disguise their heat signatures. They needed better cover and the initiative.

The guards captain weighed his weapon in his hand. He'd taken great care over his tenure at Varrdunost to obtain the best available and to stay skillful in its use, even to indulging in contests against the house guards in forbidden tests of skill and speed, but—

It would take a very well-placed shot to bring down the flyer. He would have only one, or at most, two chances. If he missed, the enemy would know precisely where they were. Gerlac focused in his eye. If he could steady his hand, there was a reasonable chance he could hit the fuel pods and explode it.

Aroused, the jungle would destroy any survivors.

Lying on soft earth, the guards captain placed his wrist on his forearm and sighted in. He must not fire, revealing his presence and his armament, until he had a clear shot. Having no hardened shelter, they would die instants after Gerlac failed to kill.

"Aurram," rumbled something altogether too close to hand.

The soldier froze.

Yvandre gathered himself together.

The flat, scaly head thrust its way through the small branches in a mighty crackling. Gerlac felt the breath sigh out of him in relief. He didn't know what it was, but he did know the flat teeth and docile gaze of an herbivore. Drawn by the kit's scent, it was a bit of needed luck.

Yvandre slithered forward, rubbed his tassels, then rubbed musky fingers beside slit nostrils, and was rewarded with a whuff of interest. The huge beast nuzzled at him. The varr motioned to Gerlac and the man came, eagerly. The creature would help conceal them.

A little later, he was less pleased by their good fortune.

If he kept close enough to be cloaked by the beast's body heat, he had to dodge clumps of dung. Too far away made the target larger, worse than nothing at all. The creature was a pipeline for masticated vegetation, slick with stomach juices.

Well, they won't find us by smell, thought Gerlac. Nose deep in a cluster of scarlet blossoms, the alert young varr looked an unlikely aesthete. They must elude the hunters until night, or Ayana, shifted the advantage to them. For the time being they must stay close to the plant-eater.

The beast was grazing its way down a steep slope, ripping whole shrubs from the ground and chewing, when there was a distant baying. The herbivore lifted its head and shat copiously, tail switching. The stench was incredible.

Nonetheless, Yvandre dropped his nosegay, flicked his tassels down, and listened, lips parted. Gerlac waited in silence until his former charge glanced at him, then queried the horizon with a gesture. The varr nodded in confirmation. There was pursuit on the ground.

There was another howl, closer, more eager. Succulent twigs and leaves trailing from its mouth, the herbivore dithered in place, treading clots of excrement. At a full chorus of hungry voices, it began to run. Yvandre sprinted after, as did Gerlac.

The drooling animal was crushing down everything in its path. With no way to escape through the intertwined branches of the thickets, they could only hope the beast's stench would cloak their scents until they reached a defensible position or a diversion.

Gerlac saved his breath for running and his eyes for the ground beneath his feet. Yvandre, younger, faster, possibly having the advantage of knowing something about the area, would have to choose their turn-off point. As a last resort, the guards captain would stop and wait, try to slow the pursuit.

The soldier saw fragments of the landscape as he ran: a wodge of earth gouged from soft soil by the beast's two-toed foot; a fallen pana fruit trapped in a net of vines and swarming with yellow bugs that exploded into flight; a landscape that suddenly opened at his feet—

They had reached the edge of a land-slip. The beast and Yvandre went over the brink without hesitation. Gerlac stopped, looked back, and saw motion in the scrub. Some of the pack were running silent. The harriers were very close.

Gene tweaked to the varr scent, thought the soldier and leaped. Wondering if, having been seen, he should take some other direction, he landed awkwardly. *No*, he thought, *I have the weapon, and must stay with the kit. If I have a chance to hand it off, then perhaps.*

Something bayed at the top of the cliff.

Gerlac ran, blindly following Yvandre, had to fend himself off the cliff-face with one arm. Panting, he looked up. Above him, already safe from immediate pursuit, the kit was hauling itself up the rock face with the strength in its arms, boots at its belt, bare feet dangling.

Good, the guards captain thought, *good*, and reached and pulled, feet scrambling for purchase. Once climbing had been had been a much-practiced skill, but now he had to concentrate on placing a hand here, foot there. The pursuit was no longer hunting silent.

Howls ringing in his ears, he heaved himself onto a ledge slightly narrower than his torso, stared down, and felt his head spin. At the cliff's base the harriers yammered, eager to rip his flesh, gnaw his bones. At his side, Yvandre snarled at the unnatural, ugly things.

Six-limbed, they ran on four, had two others to grip prey, bring it down or to their mouths. A ruff of coarse fur protected the throat and their narrow yellow eyes had a flat, fixed stare that held your gaze if you—

The varrling tapped his cheek.

"Uh," said Gerlac. It had been a decade, more, since he had suffered from prey fever, the first sight of a predator hunting you. He sat back on his heels, licking dry lips, glanced at his charge busy piling fist-sized rocks. Yvandre had a fierce half-smile. Varr enjoyed an adrenaline rush: it was one of the things that made them supremely dangerous.

But the varrling was right. The harriers would be easy targets if they attempted the sheer wall. Gerlac began to gather his own ammunition, ears tuned for noises at the top of the cliff. If he were handling the hunt, the next thing he would do, would be to come over the edge on ropes.

The beasts at the bottom of the rock began slinking through the brush, as if they had given up, gone away. You had to look closely to see the ambush around the temptingly vacant space, two here, and there a third so still it was near-invisible.

Their back trail was blocked. Man, if not varr, would be torn to shreds, and the man would be the luckier of the two. Gerlac leaned back against the stone and closed his eyes. *Just a moment's rest*, he thought. *I'm not up to this anymore.*

"Wuff," said something and a gust of fetid air washed over the soldier.

Startled, he opened his eyes, stared at the huge head, mouth bristling with greenery, level with his own. "Eerumph," belched the beast, favoring them with another blast. "Smells better than the other end," said Gerlac.

Yvandre grinned, fangs bared.

Strange sounds gone, the herbivore had reverted to its normal occupation, feeding, and had grazed back along the cliff's foot until it had ambled across its own panicky trail. It had not scented the harriers in the thickets, or perhaps it had been drawn to the varr despite the presence of the alien predators.

It chewed, dipped its head for another mouthful, chewed. In this dry season, the vegetation at the base of the cliff was a fresher green than the surrounding woods, nourished by the run-off of water and minerals from above. "Brumphh," said the beast, and tore up another shrub.

Yvandre watched with interest.

The kit is, the soldier thought, *probably hungry. Certainly I am.* The harriers, Gerlac suddenly realized, were probably kept on short rations to make them keen for their work. All of the animals in the area, being tuned to varr, might smell vaguely varr. The predators could look, but not feed.

Ravenous, though, they might kill despite the ingrained prohibition.

"Ah," said Yvandre with satisfaction as the horde below rose from their hiding places and began to stalk. The guards captain watched in tense silence, fingers clenched on a stone. The varr scanned the cliff above, one step ahead.

Small and agile, one harrier ran back and forth at the feet of the behemoth, mewling. The giant animal peered at it, lowered its head, curious. Gerlac released his grip on the rock: he had thought he might need to draw blood to provoke them. There was no need.

The lead hunter took the behemoth from the side, at the point of the jaw, and was followed by its fellows until herbivore wore a beard of writhing bodies chewing into its throat. It groaned as its spurting blood dyed its attackers, then it sank to its knees, fell flat out.

It was all over except for the gorging, interrupted by spats as the members of the pack jockeyed for the choicer bits, the eyes, the lips. *So fast,* thought the man, seeing himself there. *Already you can see bone and the tongue has been—*

Yvandre touched Gerlac's shoulder. Time for phase two, while the harriers were busy. They could not get out by going down, could not risk exposing themselves to the unknown dangers at the top. Therefore man and varr must hide on the rock itself.

The kit was leaning out, feeling for the first handhold for the climb. Gerlac reached to secure the varr's ankles. A little small stuff clattered past, knocked loose by Yvandre's scrabbling talons. The man bowed his head, and hoped his own grip would hold.

Eyes squeezed shut, shoulders tensed against blows that did not come, the soldier grimaced. "Take your time," he said softly. Eager to get out of peril, Yvandre was in no need of being told to hurry. Then was another clattering of pebbles, off to his left.

It was at moments like this he remembered his older brother's contemptuous, "Varr's-man," the last time he had been home. Young, proud of his rank, and eager to impress, Gerlac had boasted of his military training. Larin's disdain of what was the source of so much pride to him had tipped the balance.

He had sworn fealty the next day, become in truth a varr's-man for life. The guards captain expected to die in the service of the dark ones, but not today if he could help it. Dying, he had often been told, won no honor. The unmen wanted results, not martyrs.

"Uh," grunted the kit and began to lift his own weight.

Gerlac pressed himself against rock and waited.

The guards captain had three priorities: save the kit, gather information on the poachers, save himself. When Yvandre grunted success, the soldier reached up and gripped, beginning his own climb. Something gave way under his right hand, and he swung, one-armed, over the gulf.

Yvandre's naked foot was shoved into his face.

"No," the man grunted, trying to lift himself with his left hand.

Two fingers slipped free.

Hanging there, possible scenarios flashed through his mind.

One, he took the proffered help and they both fell. If he was observed, and it was just possible they were being watched by satellite link, Ayana and his unborn child would receive no help from the dark lords.

Two, he fell alone and was killed. The kit, young, strong, and skillful, would still have a good chance of getting away. Ayana and the child would be—

Yvandre hissed in fury, grabbed Gerlac's wrist with its toes, and pulled straight up. Completely off the face of the cliff, the man treaded air until he found purchase with both feet, then climbed as he had never climbed before, eyes closed, feeling his way up the rock.

Until he was gripped by guiding hands that pressed him against water-smoothed stone, eyes closed, breathing hard. He could feel sweat from his armpits running down his shirt, the thighs of his pants. At least it hadn't filled his boots.

"Ft!" said Yvandre, licking a broken talon.

"Yeah," sighed Gerlac. Near thing. "You're not to do that—"

"Ft!"

Human life was supposed to be worth nothing to the varr. "Don't do it again," the soldier said, not looking at the fanged grin, unable to put any force behind the words. He was in good shape for someone so nearly dead. Scrapes, bruises, a scratch or two. A dinged ego didn't count.

They were lodged in a water-cut pocket in the cliff-face, above and to the left of the corpse of their gigantic companion, when a wave of hot air heavy with the stink of disrupted vegetation buffeted them. Sand sifted past the opening. They looked at one another, listened.

Nothing.

Disrupter beam.

Someone in orbit had noticed what was going on. It was unlikely that their aim would be perfect. "Let's get further in," said the guards captain. There was a cool breeze from the opening at their back. It might be deep enough to save them from breathing superheated air.

Yvandre didn't bother to agree, just went. Crawling after him, the soldier stopped, hands pressed to glass-smooth floor. Whatever it was, this space was not natural. He sniffed, but there was no particular odor: it had been open for some time.

As his eyes became accustomed to the dimness, he saw it was not, as he had feared, a tomb, but a storage-place, walls lined with cases piled higher than his head, sections of the floor grooved to give traction to those who worked here. On one wall the wheel of wings, emblem of the oldest varr, was deeply incised.

Wind and weather had begun to damage the pieces nearest the opening where water had worn through. *How many years*, thought the soldier, and settled himself beneath the wheel to rest, calling, "Stay in sight," to Yvandre. With reasonable caution the kit should be safe. There shouldn't be a guardian here.

He could hear his charge rummaging around, curious.

There was an odd click-and-hum and the soldier got to his feet. "Yvandre?" No answer. "Yvandre!" He rounded a corner to face a stocky man, silver-haired, black-eyed, with a creamy gold complexion. With recognition of the famous face—Deltander, companion to one of the first Red Lords—came the knowledge it was only a simulacrum.

Yvandre crouched, intent, not having encountered one of these before. The image, which had probably been aware of the varrling as soon as it entered the chamber, if not before, depending on how its sensors were fitted, glanced at the guards captain then returned its attention to the young lord.

Gerlac's father had had helped his village exorcise one of these with rocks once, an expensive mistake. Simulacra were old, and much-desired by the dark ones. They could speak, if questioned. He'd never get the kit moving once that happened.

"Yvandre. We can come back, later."

Reluctant, the kit stood up. It was bemused, unthreatening, and yet he was suddenly acutely aware that it was fully as tall as he and far more formidable. As the young varr turned away, the image vanished. The simulacra would wait, as it had waited for hundreds of years.

The technology of that age was both fabulous and forgotten, or so it was said. Gerlac wouldn't bet on the forgotten: it was not like the dark lords to forget anything. Ever. He peered into the depths, wondering what else was concealed there, said, "Let's get out of here."

Yvandre agreed silently.

At the opening they both paused.

Tongue out, the unman tasted the air.

There was a faint scent of burning.

A silver of light raced down the sky, and the cliff shuddered. Whoever was in orbit was busy. Yvandre swung out and began to climb. Gerlac followed without a word. Whatever it had based its decision on, the varr's judgment was as likely to be good as his own. It was a time to take risks.

They came out on the near-side ridge, well beyond where guards captain had crossed it on his way into the valley. A bolt of light pierced the jungle below and steam mushroomed. There would not be much left wherever that beam touched. "Show yourself," said the soldier.

They lay on their backs, staring into the steel blue of the sky. Having waited sufficient time for an identification, Yvandre rolled over, got its legs under itself and ran. Gerlac followed. There was another whuff of green wood exploding, and a second, nearer.

Rising into the air the soldier gasped, "Yvandre," and tumbled, stunned. Conscious again, he rolled over to watch chaos erupt in the valley, glad he had not called in the strikes, necessary though they were. The unmen were going to be displeased with the state of Yost's defenses.

As for Yvandre—

"Ayana's going to be angry," Gerlac said.

The dark lord didn't even bother to shrug.

❑❐

Somewhere far to the east, the force fences had dropped, and the herds were on the move, tens, hundreds, thousands of thousands of animals moving at the steady jog that would take them across the continent in three or four ten-days.

Orbiting surveillance checked that the seasonal ponds were full where the permanent watering holes were more than a day's run apart. Only in good conditions did the pick-a-back vines, with their precious freight of seeds for the winter ground cover, survive.

⊔⊐

It was harvest-time at Varrdunost. Somewhere above the high blue sky, ships waited to be filled with the sweet-smelling kernels the po-birds were gorging on. On the ground every able-bodied person prepared for the ten-days of labor that would climax their working year.

A horde of small children in florescent red and orange ran across the road, splashed with mud to the knees from the ditch, yelling as they drove birds out of the tall grass. Their pursuing mothers, armed with bows, scarcely spared a glance for the arrival of their overlord.

One, yelling at her two mud-dappled brats, darted in front of the dark lord's mount without hesitation. Yvandre drew rein, waited for the rest. *So much for the terrors of varr rule*, thought Gerlac. Individual unmen could have horrifying idiosyncrasies, but they were seldom less than skillful guardians of their holdings.

In contrast to the bright colors of the safety-dressed children, the adults' work clothes were worn drab, but everyone looked well-fed and brisk, even the white-haired oldest driving the carts bringing supplies to the camp. What disabled and sick there were would be elsewhere, still, Gerlac looked about him with satisfaction.

As a new recruit landed on Heltarden, a border world with militias making incursions into varr space, the soldier had walked out of an unresisting spaceport to see faces that were little more than skulls with skin, a parade of walking skeletons, and half a hundred bodies rotting by the side of the road, unburied and unburned. He promptly puked on his boots.

It had never occurred to him that it was possible for whole populations to be malnourished. In that moment, the guardsman had become fiercely proud he served the dark lords. The worst the un-men did, the occasional renegade, red-handed, petty savagery, was nothing in comparison to such mass agony.

The dark ones feed everyone every day, thought Gerlac, who had been a farmer's child before he was a soldier. Jungle-gathered pharmaceuticals might be more valuable, but the foundation of the varr's ancient empire was the self-seeding grains they had designed. It would take a planetary-scale disaster before anyone starved on a varr world.

It had never happened.

Attention entirely in the here and now, Yvandre set his gray kemas caracoling, splattering filthy water everywhere, until it reached drier footing at the side of the road. Wiping a cheek, Gerlac urged his own piebald out of range, and made no comment. The kit was asserting control of its ill-tempered, intelligent mount, putting it through its paces.

The mud that fouled the ways beside streams coming down from the highlands would be the last to go. The plains had to have been dry a ten-days or so before the harvest was be declared. Damp grain fouled the equipment that lifted it to orbit, could even rot, sprout, became covered with rusts and blights before it freeze-dried in the holds.

Harrooom, haroom! Some one on the heights had spotted their party, was signaling the main camp. A turn in the road, and they reached a flat place in a curve of the creek that must flood every spring, for nothing on it grew higher than a man's knee. A half-dozen temporary huts were in place, and others were rising.

A dozen youths ran forward to hold their kemas and take their packs. That done, varr and man were granted a decent privacy from curiosity. Their shelter was nothing but four screens of sticks and straw woven into complex patterns that let the wind through, the whole topped with a thick roof of bundled grasses, but it served its purpose.

A whiff of smoke, savory with herbs, told Gerlac why the children had been chasing po-birds. *Splatchcocked, and grilled,* thought the soldier, suddenly not regretting his missed breakfast. A whiff of frying sweet-bread gusted by him, and he swallowed saliva.

Somewhere out of sight, the village elders gave a great musical sigh. Over a splatter of patting hands, they rehearsed their welcome to an outside world that they saw only at harvest. There would be gossip, and the sounds of the balbek and tibrun, deep into the purple harvest night.

❑❐

Few things besides information are worth sending rapidly across astronomical distances, but in the deeps of space, that which is shoved goes a long way, and anything safe in the great cold can be shipped. Grain, hulled and cleaned, is a staple in most star-systems.

High protein varieties are basic food in the out-colonies, the permanent habitats too far from the warm hearth of their star to grow food without additional energy. On-station, the constant need for enough high-quality calories gives urgency to the phrase, Basic Necessity.

The varr had the ships, the strains of grain, and when they had taken control of enough planets, they became merchants to many who had to buy or go hungry. If unmen fed their own worlds without thought or stint, they were not above using food as a tool of diplomacy when they dealt with feral humans.

In the end, varr-lover was a curse on a hundred worlds.

From the Introduction to The Histories of Kendre Kant.

❑❐

The bray of kemas and horns woke Gerlac. Poking his head out of the hut, he thought, *I'm probably the only one in the entire great square who slept late.* Ears throbbing to trial flurries of drumbeats, the guards captain washed his face at the stream and went to look for his varr.

It was not hard to find. Yvandre, already mounted, was marshaling the lines of villagers who would beat the big toothos-drums, driving the wild herds and their predators as they, too, were culled and harvested. Most of Varrdunost's meat for the year would be pulled down in the next few days.

Harooom! Harom! At that sound, people sorted themselves into squads and groups without any apparent direction. The drums thundered, beginning the beat that would carry them all through the long day and into the night. Harvest had begun.

❏❐

Dufan crouched in the open port, watching the green billows of Heltarden's foliage slide by below. Somewhere down there were unimaginable riches. Some leaf. Some root. Some insect. Some careless varr lord. *One's here*, he thought, gathering a loop of line into his left hand and swinging again. *Luck be with me.*

The rich-man-to-be didn't know where his fortune was hiding, and the fix at the surveillance center only gave him the briefest of windows to operate in, but today was his day. Something pale flashed in the darkness under the leaves. Gear in hand, Dufan signaled a turn, then crouched, alert.

That might have been an upturned face.

❑❒

A connector broke, spewing grain, and Gerlac watched the resulting confusion resolved with critical approval. "There," pointed the unman, and heedless of danger a dozen people ran in, latched the bore-end down, struck the faulty assembly and mounted another. It might all have been a dance to the distant boom, booma, boom.

Yvandre's exhausted mount staggered, and a second was brought alongside. The varr swung one leg over, freed the other, shifted his hips and was in the second saddle before anyone could move to help, other then by holding the new mount's cheek-straps tight. The dark lord cantered off, intent on the next latch-up.

Juvenile though it was, Yvandre's leadership was skillful and essential. Having grown up on the estate, the unman knew every squad leader, all the equipment, all the moves. The young varr was enjoying its first large-scale administrative success. It signaled for the flow to begin again.

Unneeded, Gerlac urged his kemas to a gallop, foretasting sweet freedom and bitter regret. Soon he would no longer be even nominally responsible for the kit. A shadow slid across the grain-gold fields and was gone, but the soldier, racing the wind, did not see it.

❏❐

Dufan had not planned to land, but the brilliant flash of light had damaged something in the navigation systems. If he were lucky, it would be a simple recalibrate and reset. Meanwhile, he must set down in cover, wait until the terminator brought darkness and a chance of escape without collusion.

While he waited, he would hunt, covering the metalized shell of his flyer with litter and branches so it would be less easily detected by the orbiting security that should be looking elsewhere. *Never count on things going to plan*, Dufan thought.

He still felt lucky as he checked his gear.

❏❐

This close, the beats of the toothos drums, each carried by two men and played by two others, made everyone's chest throb. Somewhere ahead of the hunt, fleeing herds of chevre and prides of ruff-cat fled, driven by the man-made thunder. A few were old enough to have run before, and were not likely to run again.

Hunters, following on Kemas and on foot, culled the obvious stragglers and begin the tagging and separation, spraying the beasts with purple, blue, and the glowing pink that was a death sentence. They gave the frightened animals time to cool, then cut the selected victims down methodically.

The skinning teams followed, doing the preliminary work on each carcass where it fell, leaving the discards to fatten the remaining predators or, dusted with quick-rots and repellents, to return to the soil immediately and increase next year's grain crop.

The hunt masters were still reading the complex lists, age and weight from the first returns, when Gerlac went in search of Yvandre, whom he found sharpening his fangs meditatively on the cartilage of a roasted rib. It had been a good day, but the young varr looked tired.

"Had enough?" the soldier said, bluntly.

Yvandre nodded, and laid the bone into the fire, where it flared into fat-yellow flame. Heavy with child, Ayana had come late and waited for them at the camp. As they made their way down the wide, deserted stair into the silence of the valley, even the wind smelled of blood.

To the east, a star fell from the earth into the heavens.

Heads down, watching their feet, neither man nor varr noticed.

Those who should have seen, were, as planned, absent.

❏❐

Refrigerated carryall thumping against his chest, Dufan reminded himself not to walk so fast to be obviously nervous nor so slow as to seem a tourist. People to whom his prize was ten years' wages, more, brushed by him on either side. He wasn't sure where to go, and speed was important.

Once he'd been able to depend on his brother to keep track of dealers, but now Harrie only supplied the capital and took half the profits. Unstinting financial support was no replacement for an active on-the-ground partner. With the haul of a lifetime, Dufan no time to waste.

He squared his shoulders against the pull of the harness and palmed the let-me-enter of a security door. Air hissing around him, the poacher was propelled, slightly off-balance by design, into the outer office of Desines and Companions, Traders in Rare Goods.

ᗑᗕ

The flyer joggled constantly over the rough ground, which was tiring. Gerlac leaned to the window, wishing they would be over the water crossing soon: he wanted to sleep or at least pretend to.

He and Yvandre were on their way to Varrdunost after a last end-of-harvest reconnaissance before the young varr answered Beltar's long-awaited summons. The Red Lord had, advertently or inadvertently, given Yesdar's heir every opportunity to mature but the time when it must appear before the council and be tested had finally come.

If things went extremely well, Yvandre would be accepted and would return for more years of learning to run its vast holdings—the old lord had held three planets in thrall—beginning the climb to its sire's seat on the council of the dark lords, as arbiter of varr relations with mankind.

Should they go less well, the young varr would begin its probably-brief career as a diplomat to human space, a discardable pawn in interstellar politics, with little hope of a permanent return to the centers of power. Some other lord or lords would be eager to manage its unsecured holdings while waiting for its death.

Yvandre's face as he watched the landscape beneath was composed, impossible to read. Knowing the odds, and the difficulty doing anything that might tilt them now, it might have dismissed the matter from its thoughts. Or perhaps not. It had a pensive expression.

Gerlac, exhausted from trying to think of every possible precaution and warning, had finally dozed off in his seat. Awakened by the whump and blinding flash of an exploding power source he thought, *Sabotage*, even as their craft skimmed into the side of a mountain.

It came to rest nose down in a silence more shocking than the cacophony of shrieking metal grinding over rock that had preceded it. Half-blinded by blood, the guards captain felt about, encountering a tangled, slimy mass that was enough to tell him the pilot must be dead. His young lord's place was empty.

"Yvan—"

"Sst," said something at his ear and clawed hands pulled at him.

Gerlac followed their urgent summons, tumbled through a gap in the shattered hull. On his back in snow, helmet askew, he had a confused impression of whirling clouds and dark smoke before the varr threw itself on him and shoved off.

The man felt an icy rush down his back. They were sliding fast and he was the sled. They went airborne for an instant, and the soldier saw patches of darkness at impact. An enormous pulse of light and sound passed above them, and ringing silence returned.

The flyer had blown up.

Gerlac got himself sitting and looked around.

Bleeding from a cut over one eye, Yvandre was brushing snow off of himself with fastidious casualness. All around their tumbled patch of white the snow was dark with soot and debris. The outcropping they had gone over had saved them from being fragged by metal and ceramic.

The human was not stupid enough to think they were in the only shelter with the radius of the blast by accident. The varr got painfully to its feet, and

Gerlac did the same. When it looked around, then staggered down slope, the man followed unquestioningly.

Muddled by sleep and shock, he had assumed that it was winter wherever they had crashed. They were moving through a silvery mist when Gerlac saw spikes of green growth on scrub trees and understood. The crash had been above the permanent snowline. If they descended far enough fast enough they would not freeze.

Propelled by gravity, they moved quickly despite bruises and strains. The cloud-veiled sun was still above the high horizon, when Gerlac smelled jungle. Sniffing the wind, Yvandre stopped, considered, and changed course. The mist grew heavier, covering them with chill dew.

Immense tree trunks, branches draped with vines and epiphytes, loomed and faded as they passed. Gerlac's eye traced one curve, followed it to another. They were among overgrown ruins. "Where is this?" he asked, voice loud in the leaf-shrouded silence.

Yvandre shrugged, How-would-I-know.

The man's mouth went dry. Deserted cities of the varr were seldom truly deserted, and what had stayed behind in them had never been friendly to humans. "Yva—" He stopped, appalled by his shrill voice. Silently, he started repeating, *You're with it, you're all right*, as he walked.

The sun was sinking into a steaming gold and purple twilight, when Yvandre came to a path whose paving was worn comparatively clean by the passage of many feet. Or perhaps only a few feet, day after day, for the cleared strip was narrow, and the moss on either side undisturbed.

A rush of something with a long-winged, delicate silhouette against the ruddy sunset sky made Gerlac jump. He couldn't tell its color, but he was sure it was a flame-cock. Seeing that, he would rather have been huddled in the sterile cold of the high slopes. "Wit, wit," said something in a treetop.

It was answered, "Wit, wit, wit." The soldier took a deep, reluctant breath. Shipan. Ootorono was nothing compared to the seething ecology experiment of Yost's notorious, carefully isolated, lowland. Even the dark ones were careful here, wary of the results of uncontrolled change.

"Churr," called the varr, and the jungle went silent.

Its fiercest predator was back.

Gerlac licked nervous lips, not happy Yvandre was advertising their presence. Something not very far away boomed. "Wit, wit, wit," gabbled dozens of flame-cocks. The soldier rubbed the tight spot at his sternum, thinking, *Be calm*. "Ooom." The leaves on nearby trees quivered at the sound.

The booming shifted from hopeful to mournful as the last of the light faded. They followed the pale ribbon of the foot-cleared path through the undergrowth. The varr, of course, could still see where he was going, but Gerlac followed only the sensation of darkness, of body heat, immediately ahead.

"Chrt?" said the varr.

"Ooom?" queried that immense voice—

It had him before he saw it coming, a slimy tongue as big as a man. Smothered in smooth flesh, the soldier struggled fiercely to reach his weapon, was poked somewhere, sealed in. Hearing the varr's contented churr somewhere near in the folds of membranes, Gerlac stopped thrashing.

"Ooom!"

He felt like his eardrums were bleeding.

"Chrt," said the varr, very softly.

Summarily dumped onto an oozy surface, blind in the dark, he fumbled about until he touched Yvandre, who settled against him, back to back, and drowsed off immediately. The soldier wished he could do the same. The close air stank and his head ached abominably.

The guards captain was uncertain when he slept and when he dreamed until light woke him. They were inside a translucent ivory shell, at the moment uninhabited by anything other than themselves. Like the satiny interior, the soldier's clothes were glossy with mucus.

We're alive, he thought, and peering out the opening at the trail of glistening slime marked where their host had cruised off in search of breakfast or—there was a tremendous splash not far away—to drink, bath, or absorb water. Gerlac rolled out and got to his feet, ignoring stiff muscles and bruised bones

The sooner they were out of here, the better. The guards captain was eager to find some clearing from which they might signal the ever-watchful satellites. *If*, the soldier thought with sudden cynicism, *they are still watching.* The brilliant blue sky should be dotted with searchers and, as far as he could see, there was nothing.

The varr poked its head out—yawned, slotting teeth out and in—got to its feet. Yvandre considered a dozen flies, sluggish in the cool morning air, circling over a pile of rasped-clean bone fragments and, without further preliminaries, started upslope.

Off the path, the terrain was rugged, with knobs of rock poking up though the litter under the trees. The dark lord stepped on stone preferentially, although if it was because it gave the best footing or to avoid some unknown hazard of the forest floor, the man did not know.

He did the same.

They broke out of the tall trees toward midafternoon, coming out on a shelf of granite that overlooked the next valley. If they were going to have to camp another night, under its overhang was a good place to stop. The edges of the lightening-glazed stone were overhung by thorny bushes, heavy with thumb-sized yellow fruit.

The varr pulled and nibbled a few. Gerlac, not so dedicated a carnivore, filled himself with the sweet, near-flavorless pulp. Full, the man stretched beside the varr in the shade. They should spread a signal in the open space above. Neither of them mentioned it.

There was no telling who was watching.

Yvandre was at an inconvenient, competent age. The man watched the varr watch until its attention became fixed on a distant patch of glitter. Wet foliage, thought Gerlac, reflecting sunlight, or perhaps shiny leaves or fronds. Still, the dark lord watched with fierce intensity.

❑❐

The ruff-cat sniffed the smooth curve. Men had been here, at dawn perhaps, or a little before, the scent fading with the heat of day. The cat sniffed again, uneasy, lifted a leg, pissed on the odd object, and, mouth open, nose crinkled, judged the result. It still stank foreignness.

He was hungry and the herds of hartebuck would be moving to shelter from the noonday sun. Designed-in instincts at odds with the natural ones, the ruff-cat switched his tail, crouched down, sniffed again.

The breeze brought a whiff of fresh dung and cropped green leaves. Ducking under a canopy of foliage the lithe, green-eyed shadow crept uphill. Later would be soon enough to deal with the alien object. There was prey not ten body-lengths away.

❑❒

Brooding, Gerlac watched the flyer glide down the grassy landing strip. They'd been lifted out minutes after they had settled on the ridge. Although it had said nothing, Yvandre was clearly less than pleased that their adventure had been truncated.

The unman was going to be even less pleased when it discovered the guards captain had countermanded its orders that the valley be searched thoroughly on the ground. Yost's unseasoned security forces were too terrified to do the job. In a moment or two it would ask—

Yvandre, eyes narrowed, looked up from his conference.

Its chair fall backwards.

Then it was in front of him, stinking with rage.

It knows, thought Gerlac and threw himself backward, leaving throat and belly undefended. He'd thought he'd have a moment or two to explain; he'd thought wrong. Arm across his face, he lay on his back. After a long time, when no claws tore at him, the man let his arm fall away.

To find himself staring full into the face of the crouching varr. Yvandre touched his throat with clawed fingers, then rose and walked a deliberate back-turned-to-you two paces away and faced the supine man again. Within seconds of dying, the soldier, told himself, *Don't move.*

An eternity passed.

Gerlac looked away and slowly sat up. When that drew no response, he got to his knees and got one foot under him. *I was stupid*, he thought. Eyes cold, his former charge reached for him with perfect deliberation. The soldier held still for what was coming.

The pain was agonizing. Blood running down his ripped cheek, the guards captain bowed his balding head. He'd been foolish to presume on their years as a family. For a planetary lord, letting its orders be countermanded by another varr, let alone a mere human, was suicidal.

Yvandre was in the right.

Hand to his face, blind with tears, Gerlac left the courtyard.

No matter what Beltar said, his guardianship had ended.

❏❐

Amadora Desines, son of the founder, looked up from his desk, appraised Dufan's shabby clothes, heavy harness, and determined and belligerent expression, then waved a senior trader to his service. The trader babbled his name and a greeting, bowed the new client to a booth, drew the door, and waited expectantly.

Checking his surroundings for surveillance, certain it was there although he could not see it, Dufan worked the straps off his shoulders. Unshackling the bag, he put it dead center on the impervious shelf that served as a table.

Slightly hollowed, so anything that spilled could be saved to the last grain, the surface would automatically signal density and weight, both irrelevant to the current transaction. From force of habit, Desines' trader glanced at the display before shutting it down.

Dufan tapped the control, and the carryall opened like an eight-petaled flower, forming a ruff around the head. The eyelids of the pale alien face fluttered. The lips moved. There was no sound, for there was no voice box, and no breath to power it if there had been, but it was alive.

"Wonderful," breathed the trader, then looked as if he wished he had not spoken.

Dufan remained silent: his goods proclaimed their value.

"Fifty thousand," suggested the trader.

Dufan tapped the control, and the petals began rising. Drug-unfocused eyes twitched back and forth in their sockets. Separated from its heart, lungs, and other support systems, the brain could go mad but it could not die of shock. There might be a chance of forcing the varrling to communicate.

"Sixty-five," offered the trader, as the case latched.

"One hundred," said Dufan flatly, "and security to get me to my ship."

You couldn't count on a capture surviving. A clean kill of a fresh prey, quick stripping, and careful connections to the equipment he'd custom-designed and things still went wrong. This was the first he managed to get to a dealer in such prime condition.

Desines would pay his price.

They couldn't afford not to.

Their corporate prestige was on the line.

❑◻

Planetary surface turning into landscape as they descended below local traffic patterns, Gerlac stripped the latest intelligence off a drone satellite, silently cursed Beltar, then tiredly said some choice things about local defense aloud. His remarks might get back to where they would do some good.

Two unknown craft in as many days. The council lord had made a radical misjudgment in allowing human traffic so close to a varr world. Yost security was neither quick, nor well-trained. Half were novices just learning the moves; the other half were veterans who had forgotten them.

He archived a copy of the data at Varrdunost. Later, and less publicly, would be the time to react to it. Given how close the border was, it was inevitable that some hot-head try to raid Yost and scoop up the treasures the dark lords supposedly left lying around for deserving thieves.

Not that the closeness didn't have its uses. There was some legitimate trade. Yost-raised, Yvandre was developing a nice judgment of who to pressure and who to bribe as it interacted with a feral humanity that Beltar endured only as necessary. Once proclaimed, the young lord would be priceless to its kind.

It was not clear that the Red Lord understood that. Beltar was accustomed to losing more than half of the young, and was not inclined to look into the reasons for the losses too closely. Varrlings naive or unlucky enough to be killed were considered no loss.

Waste, thought the soldier, and broke his link with a snap, knowing he was foolish to apply human standards to the dark lords' behavior. Take Yvandre. Close thought they were, Gerlac had barely gotten away with one misstep. The planetary lord-to-be was inclined to stand on his dignity and rightly so.

I'll be back on active duty soon, the guards captain thought, running through the list of things he needed to have done. It might be wise to have his artificial eye upgraded. The newer models—there was a braking rumble and his hands gripped the armrests—were capable of night vision with much finer detail.

He'd gone off-world to argue that one of the shell-ships should come to take Yost's yet-to-be-proclaimed lord safely to its testing. There had been too many young varr lost recently nearby. Nearby in astronomical terms, it was true, but nearby. A shell-ship would protect it.

Now this, the soldier thought. There had been no reports from Varrdunost for the better part of a day. Estate security might just be sloppy, but he'd fragged them verbally often enough. At the least the communications staff should have kept up the appearance of doing their duty.

Gerlac glanced at the timer, forced tense muscles to relax. Only a few more minutes. He had brought heavy-duty reinforcements with him and was taking the unusual step of landing them at Varrdunost rather than Yost-port. They would storm the place like an enemy fortress, scare everyone witless.

He hoped.

"Sir!"

"Yes?"

"The blurt announcing our arrival has not been acknowledged, sir."

"Assume hostile," said the guards captain.

"Listen! Assume hostile conditions on—" The door closed behind her, giving Gerlac a last moment of privacy, if you did not count the landing-

absorbed pilot. He could hear the officer taking her troops through the debarkation drill. "Power up," said her muffled voice.

One bump, two, and they were on the ground, pouring out onto the grassy landing strip as if taking it in a war zone. "Groups! Shields! Targets!" snapped someone and the air stank of ozone. The guards captain powered up, then, unable to wait for the formation, loped ahead.

By the time he passed the weather-worn statue, he was running. Up the path between the trees, to the main house courtyard—he stopped, panting. There was nothing obviously wrong, other than no one was there. On impulse, he went through the main door, turned left.

In the dining hall, the table was set for second meal. The pots on the kitchen stoves held soup, stew, sweet rice. There were bowls of garnishes, baskets of bread on the scrubbed-clean chopping blocks. The pantry was in order. The cold room held nothing but frosted carcasses.

Right before local noon, he thought. *Four hours or so ago*. That was when whatever had happened had happened. "Anybody here?" he called. No one answered. "It's Gerlac!" He headed through the main hall toward the storage rooms beyond. It was just possible they had needed to pack some rush shipment—

"Sir?" said a voice at his back.

He startled violently.

It was the squad leader, powered weapon poised in casual hand.

"Go over the place in pairs," the guards captain said. "There should be half a hundred people here. Find them."

"Sir." Wheeling about, she barked orders and her troops fanned out.

Gerlac powered his own weapon to maximum and jogged toward Pana Lodge, thinking, *Don't scare Ayana.* She was a few weeks from term, enormous, and nervous. The prospective father slowed down, calming himself, then he stopped.

The jungle was too quiet. When he moved, The soldier could hear his footfall echo off the rocks by the stream. He began running again, sounding like a multitude, thinking, *I should have waited for the others.* Leaping sideways, ready to fire, Gerlac burst into the open—

Flies boomed up into the cloudless blue sky.

He had found them. Varrdunost's people had been driven into the peaceful courtyard and slaughtered under the pana tree. Brought forward one by one to have their throats cut and be thrown on the heap of the dead. The air stank of terror: piss, vomit, dung, and blood.

Saved their ammunition, thought Gerlac, pulling the bodies this way, that, until he was satisfied that neither Yvandre not Ayana was among them. Numb, he switched on his link, said tersely, "Found them," on the troop frequency. There was a gabble of questions as he shut it off. Let them come and see for themselves.

He couldn't bear to describe it.

If the raiders hadn't despoiled the main house, they had done a thorough job on the lodge. From the battered floor, the golden screen had been ripped free and beaten into a compact mass. Someone had gouged the eyes of the mural's varr, slashed their crotches: it was an old superstition.

Please, he thought, searching his home, every room upstairs, then with less hope, all of those down. "Ayana?" he said, then in a whisper, "Yvandre?" They would stay hidden until they were sure who was looking for them. "It's me. Gerlac." There was no answer.

Bread had overrisen on the kitchen table, and the oven, left too long hot and empty, smelled scorched. He switched it off, turned around, almost seeing Ayana slapping the round, brown bottoms of the unbaked loaves before she went to—

Something.

There might have been time to get out the back and hide, he told himself. The woman was no good in the woods, and heavy with child besides, but with even the slightest warning, the varr might have gotten them both away. Training and instinct might have conspired to make Yvandre act without fully knowing why.

It was the flies that told him where Ayana was, the drone of hundreds at their feeding. There were bloody paw prints about the body, but whatever made them must have fled when he burst into the courtyard. He sank down on one knee, head swimming.

Whoever had killed her had taken their time, stripped her, probably raped her, although, since they had also satisfied their curiosity by cutting her unborn child from her womb, it would take expert to be sure of that. The scavengers had been at the child, too.

Unable to stop himself, Gerlac turned the tiny, gnawed bones over. There wasn't enough left to tell by visual inspection, but he'd hoped for a son to take the kit's place in his heart. A daughter, later, when he was more civilized himself. He lifted the small skull in his hand, put it down next to the rest of the bones.

The sex was to have been a surprise. Ayana had wanted to carry this one to term undisturbed in her own body. She had, perhaps, been asserting how different humans were from varr. Gerlac turned aside and vomited until he could do nothing but heave.

When he could stand, he turned his weapon on the puddle, the child, the woman, charred them to a patch on the paving that sun and wind and rain would erase. There was no point in learning what the bodies might have told him, he was witness to enough.

He still hadn't found Yvandre.

The guards captain searched the garden, beating down the flowers, thrashing through the bushes where his charge had hidden as a kit, hoping to find nothing, and yet as methodical as if his life depended on Yvandre being in the manicured tangles of the walled grounds.

There were voices calling when Gerlac finished. Unwilling to face them, he leaped, hooked one hand on the back wall, and pulled himself over. The varrling, strictly forbidden to do this, exited this way as often as it hoped to get away with it, rather than through the monitored forest gate.

The others would deal with the crime scene better than he could. With luck, he might find Yvandre alive, even unharmed. The unnaturally-silent forest closed around the hunter. Hoping the varr had fled into the wilderness, the man followed.

He could not bear to think of the alternative, that they had captured Yvandre.

❑❒

Dufan accepted the proffered credit chit. He had little respect for the traders, and less for men who wore bracelets of varr hair and perfumes from varr glands to enhance their virility, but hunting was a better living than he could make at anything else and the dark ones were worthy prey.

"Come again," said the trader.

"I will," said Dufan.

Once the first died, they'd be eager for another and he had a tip it was time for the most recent batch of young unmen to make their first solo expeditions. Varrlings were usually under-trained and overconfident and he should be able to bag one quickly.

❏❐

Purple throat pulsing, a lizard called in the dappled stillness. Something moving to a daytime hiding place. Gerlac lifted his face from the stream, trying to hear what had alarmed it. It might be what he sought. It might not. He had yet to find anything that confirmed Yvandre was alive.

The soldier sat back on his haunches.

The varrling had vanished, leaving no footprint, no claw mark, nothing. Yet, despite days of fruitless searching, he felt it was here, hidden in the forest, not taken or slain. Without some evidence to cite, Gerlac was afraid that if he returned and asked for help his request would be dismissed.

At best, the search would be passed to other hands.

Gerlac had stayed out, deliberately left sign, hoping that Yvandre would know who he was, and knowing, come to him. It had been almost three ten-days, and they had been hard. Filthy, he scrubbed bearded cheeks with wet hands, fisted his armpits, certain the damn varr could smell him coming.

He thought he'd scented it, once or twice, in the beginning. It watched him or at least was aware of where he was. That it stayed hidden could be an excess of caution, the hunting game varr played for life-and-death stakes, or a sign that Yvandre had snapped, gone wild. As the days passed, the odds of its being the last increased.

Years of work wasted if that had happened.

Gerlac bent and drank again.

It was a dry run up along the ridges to the west, and he'd swept them only yesterday, but the un-man must kill and feed sometime. The upland dengue-deer were herding under the pana trees at this season. At worst, he'd bag a roast for himself.

❏❐

With careful, indecent haste the trader carried his purchase to the lab over the trading quarters. "Varr head. Moving eyelids, mouth," he said as he came through the door. "It's the best I've ever seen." He put his burden onto the lab bench that was always ready, stepped out of the way.

"Leave," said the technician, powering up life supports. "I have to sterilize the area." He added, "I'll put it on the in-house monitor. Tell Desines," he started up a mixer, "and tell everyone to stay out. That includes him."

The trader left more quickly that he had come. It wouldn't do to give Irric anything to blame failure on. The house would make back its credits even if the experiment failed, but Desines would satisfy a client with a long memory and influence, if they had any sort of success.

A quarter shift later the senior trader listened to the cursing as the staff watched the last spatter of electrical activity fade. Their expensive hunk of meat was technically alive, but the mind it had sheltered was gone forever. The display flicked out. Irric had given up.

"Chill it," said Desines. "Strip it tomorrow."

Office tittle-tattle said the house had been offered ten million credits if they had a head that talked, however briefly. The rewards for developing a way to force the dark lords to reveal their secrets were far greater than that, but the client was bearing the expenses of the search and was willing to pay in cash.

Win or lose, Desines profited.

⌐¬

It was a fresh kill: blood still flowed from the severed neck vein and flies hadn't gathered. Gerlac examined the sandy, shelving bank. Nothing. He sniffed. Nothing but blood in the air, either. "Whoa, who, who?" called a ghost salamander from inside a log, voice echoing through the trees.

The unman had come from above, killed in the water, and fled up, too, when its pursuer rose out of cover downstream, alerted by the flush of pink in the water to try a fast push toward it. The soldier backed into an open space. Gone rogue, the varr might think killing the man was just another part of the game.

After almost a season among the broken bones of the hills, searching for something wilder than he could ever be, Gerlac had a respect for the feral dark lord he had never had for the kit he had taught to fence and track. When, if, they met it would be as strangers.

The varr could kill him and so far it hadn't. That was the only thing that gave the guards captain hope of recovering it. Truth was, he'd keep on hunting even if he had no hope. His task was a last labor of love and a self-punishment. If he'd not been away—

But he'd thought those thoughts too often.

There, the soldier thought, *that branch*.

He waded into the water and leaped.

Gerlac had one advantage. Yvandre, dense-boned like all varr, was the heavier of the two. Wherever the unman had gone, the man should be able to follow. Joints cracking, the soldier hauled himself up, and looked at what his fingers had already told him.

There were claw marks on the upper surface of the branch.

❑❒

Outside the window, the silver ribbon of the Symerill was a scribble across forest. The tourist plug droned, unheeded, in his ear as he entered notes. Off-planet luxuries delivered, Dufan was taking the scenic ride, down the spine of Yost's main continent, over the outer islands, to a final to-orbit boost over the turquoise of the central sea.

Near-certain he had gotten a valid tip, he was scouting the lay of the land in the guise as a casual visitor topping off a good deal with a little pleasure. There was not going to be much real pleasure: getting the information had stripped him of his profit for this trip and more.

If the man had not been afraid to linger, he would have demanded even more. Renegade varr servitors were not naive, even if they preferred not to be explicit as to what the transaction was about. Given the dark one's ideas of punishment, you could not blame them.

❑❐

It was a stiff climb, and his stentorian breathing must have scared everything in the high gallery of the forest away, but Gerlac doggedly followed the sticky scratches where something lithe, heavy, and clawed had gripped its way up the bark. Throwing his head back, he sniffed, smelling varr, close and angry.

The man came out of the gloom and into the sunlight, above a cloud of newly-inflated symbionts drifting from blossom to blossom. The guards captain stopped again, measuring distances, guessing preferences. There, his training said, but there, said intuition. He reached for the unmarred branch.

Swinging himself over, Gerlac could feel extra weight further out. He hoped the limb could bear both of them. "'vandre?" he said. "It's me, Gerlac." The soldier inched forward, eyes on his goal. The bunched green leaves ahead watched him intently.

A sleeping-cage, thought the man. *Small branches tied together into a nest of sorts*. The varr would unmake this one and go to a new location every night. Good enough to hide from someone on the ground, up close it was obviously unnatural.

Gerlac reached in, and flinched as teeth closed on his hand. "Yvandre," he said, patiently. "Let go." Dizzy with pain, he made the error of looking down. It was not a fall one could make and survive. Wind rustled the leaves and the branches swayed. "Uh," he said, and felt himself slip. His bleeding hand wouldn't close.

"Yvandre," he whispered, "Yvandre, I need help."

Knot of vines cut through by a claw, the leaves sprang apart. The varr glared at the man staring at the scarlet symbionts drifting below. *Poisonous*, thought Gerlac, feeling the blood drip off his hand. *That's why they are so conspicuous. They're poisonous*.

"Xth," said Yvandre, exasperated.

"Uh," said Gerlac leaning forward to press his spinning head against rough bark.

It was a lot harder getting down than getting up. His hand hurt abominably, and Yvandre showed a disposition to scramble away once it had gotten Gerlac near the ground. Given the varr's long-toed, gripping feet and sense of balance, the man stood no chance in a chase through the treetops.

On the ground, free to sit, head between his knees while the world swam around him, Gerlac gripped the varr's arm with his good hand in a punitive relinking to humanity then started to laugh at the idiocy of it all.

Yvandre stared at him as if he were completely mad.

❏❐

They were quite courteous about it, which was why Dufan didn't catch on immediately, asking him to accompany them for a check of his luggage which might have been damaged. They had kept up the pretext until he saw his dissected bags.

The door thunked solidly behind them as he turned to protest. He was alone, trapped, and by the pile of components sitting by the case, they had taken his list completely apart and drained it of its contents. He had absolutely no deniability.

❏❐

Gerlac had never considered what would happen when he brought the kit in. He had assumed, in his stunned state, that if he did bring back Yvandre, it would be his task to rebuild a life of sorts without Ayana and give the varrling some time to recover before it was tested.

So when he saw the guards he had brought close around Yvandre, the soldier felt himself unreasonably punished, even for stupidity. Beltar could not blame him for failing to do his job well, he hadn't been here when it happened, and he was not responsible for planet-wide security.

Still, the last hope died within him. He was alone, and he'd been so foolish as to get used to something else. Worse, the kit had retrogressed. Always reluctant to speak, like most of its kind, it now refused to do so at all. He had barely been able to win a gesture or two from it.

❏❐

Dufan crouched, as much from instinct as from thought, trying to orient himself without his head showing above the cover of tall grass. He had been given a few hours in which to build up a lead. Those pursuing him did not like to have the game end too quickly.

The interrogators had drained his mind as they had drained his list, learning every connection, act, plan he had or had once had. That done, the guardsmen had gone away, and the hunt master had come, explained the rules of the game as if reviewing something everyone knew.

Then he offered Dufan the chance to be the prey. Should the trader stay free for three days, he would be taken to the port, recompensed for his goods, deported, and instructed not to return. Should he fail—

The rest could remain unsaid. If they caught him, he would die, but even that would be quicker than rotting in prison, lab rat for whatever techniques varr security wanted to test. Dufan accepted. He had some skill in the jungle, and who knew, his luck might be back.

He might grow wings and learn to fly, too.

❏❐

Gerlac swung, saw the splatter of mock blood that told him he had struck deep enough, swung again nonetheless and took the top of the hacking post clear off. The painted head that bounced in the dirt was no more expressionless than his own.

He wiped his blade with practiced care.

Next they would do belly-ripping, at which he also excelled. Old as he was, the guards captain was as fit as he had ever been, ready to go into the field and do battle. Expected to do well, make up most of the years he had lost on detached duty, he never talked about his past.

Some old disgrace, perhaps, finally forgiven.

Numb with grief for things as they might have been, for Ayana, and the child unborn, and for the young varr who had almost been his friend, Gerlac had no fear of dying and little of pain. With all his willpower he molded himself into the perfect soldier, deadly and obedient.

He was entirely the dark lords'.

❑❒

The ruff-cat sniffed the carcass sprawled among the canes disdainfully. Varr-kill. It was the smaller scavengers, unengineered and so undeterred by the dark lords' scent, that would deal with this body. This time tomorrow it would be bones; in a few days there would be nothing.

❑❒

Gerlac had come to stand among the restless crowd that strained to see and hear the formal proclamation of new adult varr. The guards captain was certain the kit was already dead, name lost, forgotten, and he stood at the fringe of the crowd, where he could leave discreetly when they came to the end of the roll-call.

The wind was gay with petals stripped from the trees, nature adding festivity to an occasion deliberately low-key: there were many varrlings who would never answer to their names again, their bodies disposed of without ceremony, as was the dark lords' custom.

They came onto the platform in a group, spacing themselves out at the direction of the estate steward. The ceremony was never rehearsed. Once proclaimed, all the power of their kind would stand behind them, but until that moment they were vulnerable. Late-minute assassinations had happened.

"Uh," gasped Gerlac. Those around him glanced, startled, at the older man then looked away, having their own strong emotions to deal with, perhaps. Blood thundering in his ears, he squared his shoulders, scarcely able to breathe. *It can't be*, he told himself.

With normal vision the soldier could not have seen the individual features of the varr on the platform, but he focused his artificial eye—it took three tries, he was so excited—then was sure. Yvandre was one of the five being proclaimed today.

For all the work they had done together, his kit was an unlikely survivor. Nonetheless, there the lord-to-be-proclaimed of Yost was as arrogantly remote as its peers except that its eyes were methodically searching the sea of faces. *For me*, realized Gerlac. *For me*.

At this distance the crowd would be nothing but a mass of colors sprinkled with black-and-white uniforms. Still, the young varr searched with fierce determination, re-scrutinizing the area where Gerlac stood, knowing it had almost seen something and uncertain what.

Trembling, Gerlac stepped back into the open, tilted his head so sunlight would catch the livid scar the varr had cut on his cheek. It was as if a thread of fire leaped across the heads of hundreds.

Deaf and blind to the rest of the world, varr and man gazed at one another as the ceremony went forward.

In the course of things, they would not meet again, but they knew one another. At that moment, it almost seemed enough. Gerlac let the wind dry the tears on his cheeks, indifferent to curious stares.

He wandered away at random, came out onto a great terrace above a water garden, and stopped, blinded by the glittering glare. He had not meant to come here. The place was too significant to him. There, up that flight of stairs, had been Yesdar's quarters.

A very young guards captain had paused here, shaken by his responsibility, before hurrying an unwanted kit out of danger. He touched the balustrade with one finger, thinking, I had no idea how right I was to be scared. A wiser man—

I never wanted to be wise, thought Gerlac watching the light on the water, bright and insubstantial as hope. Hands gripping stone, he wished that Ayana were there. It had been more than a year, yet sometimes he thought—

"Gerlass," said a husky voice, mispronouncing his name as she had.

"Yvandre," said the man absently, to his memories. Then, seeing the reality, the robe, lance and orb, he knelt, eyes on the paving. "Yost Lord," he added, stunned. Beltar had acted swiftly.

A taloned hand tilted his chin up. Newly-proclaimed and invested, the dark lord carried the regalia of office with élan, but its narrow silver stare held a hint of amusement. It was glad to see him. Fangs gleamed as it smiled.

It touched the soldier's shoulder, paused.

"Yes," said the guards captain.

At that, his hard-worn insignia shredded in sharp claws. No longer did he serve the varr. Yost had claimed him for its own. "Pyrrin," Gerlac said, slowly getting to his feet.

"Come," said Yvandre and together they went up the stairs.

The End

www.ingramcontent.com/pod-product-compliance
Lightning Source LLC
Chambersburg PA
CBHW020139180626
46810CB00004B/1638